MW01180954

Whitney G.

This is a work of fiction. Names, characters, places, and incidents either are the product of the author's imagination or are used fictitiously, and any resemblance to actual persons, living or dead, business establishments, events, or locales is entirely coincidental.

Copyright © 2016 by Whitney Gracia Williams.

This title was previously published as "My Last Resolution: A Novella" Copyright © 2015

All rights reserved. No part of this book may be reproduced, stored in a retrieval system, or transmitted in any form, or by any means, electronic, mechanical, photocopying, recording or otherwise without prior permission of the author.

Cover design by Najla Qamber of Najla Qamber Designs

For Tamisha Draper.
How you put up with me as your BFF I'll never know...
Thanks for keeping me in line (Or trying to...LOL)

Prologue

Eleven.

Not ten. Not twenty. *Eleven.*

Ever since I was a little girl, my mom would force my sister and me to list our resolutions at the end of the year. She'd tell us to fold them up and carry them in our pockets as a reminder, and to make sure that the last one ("lucky number eleven") was the most important one of all.

I never understood the purpose behind those resolutions, and in the early years, I'd do it just to make her shut up. I'd write things like: "Stop telling Mom that she gets on my nerves." "Learn how to dropkick the boy who always pops my bra straps." "Steal better snacks from the cafeteria at lunchtime."

Yet, as the years passed and I entered high school, I started to take them a little more seriously: "Lose lots and lots of weight by the summer." "Try to work on my writing every day." "Stop trying to fit in so much and just be myself." And I always looked forward to writing that number eleven. Although it was supposed to be a goal, mine was more like a dream: "Find a real life bad boy, make him fall in love with me, and live wild and carefree together for the rest of our lives."

Unfortunately, I didn't find him in high school. That "lots and lots of weight" took way too long to lose, and the lames that came shortly after were only interested in having sex.

Very, very bad sex.

My real life bad boy stormed into my life during my senior year of college, in the form of a sweet-talking, former womanizing, ultimate-alpha-male-sweetheart named Adrian Smith, III. After preventing me from nearly walking into a moving bus, he told me I was "the sexiest woman [he'd] ever seen," and the rest was history.

Our love affair was fast and frantic, uncontrollable and overwhelming; it was so reckless and volatile that it almost became an obsession.

I fell in love with him after only a few weeks, but I knew he was the man I wanted to spend the rest of my life with.

He was my dream.

My number eleven.

After we graduated college—when things began to slow down and settle, we decided to stay together for the long haul. We had separate goals and aspirations, so we promised to strive for them while still hanging onto each other.

Unfortunately, that's where the nice version of my story ended.

My life with Mr. Bad Boy became more of a tragedy than a love story. And at the end of last year, I did something I hadn't done in years...

I changed my number eleven.

Chapter 1

Fuck it. I can't do this shit anymore...

I roll over in bed and look at the man who's sleeping next to me. My current boyfriend and winner of America's Top Asshole Award: Adrian Smith, III.

He's honestly a vision—chestnut brown hair, perfectly chiseled jawline, and a smile that can charm any woman into doing whatever he wants. He's gorgeous, even when he isn't trying to be, but for the past few months (Okay, okay...*years*), I've hated the very sight of him.

"Something wrong, Paris?" He opens his light brown eyes.

"No."

"Are you sure?"

No! "Yeah, I'm sure."

"Are you still upset with me about the grad school thing?"

"Why would I be upset about the *grad school thing*?" I try my best to sound as nonchalant as possible.

"Aw. Come here, babe..." He sits up and motions for me to lay against his chest, but I don't move.

I'm not interested in cuddling and I am beyond upset.

"Okay..." He sighs. "I know you're mad right now, but I think you'll see where I'm coming from six months from now. I have your best interests at heart and you know it. I always do."

I tune him out and focus on the broken clock that stands across the room. I've heard this speech so many times that I can spit it out verbatim: "I know how much you sacrificed for me all those years and I appreciate it, but..."

There's always a "but"...

"And that's all I'm saying." He leans over and kisses me once he finishes his speech, breaking me out of my thoughts. "Why aren't you happy about getting engaged anymore? I haven't seen you smiling in a while."

"I *am* happy about getting engaged." I lie, wincing at the very thought of being married to him, of accepting the gaudy ring that's sitting on top of our dresser.

"Good. You should be even happier now that I'll have bigger paychecks coming in. Soon, we won't have to be like every other struggling couple."

"I can't wait..." I suppress a major eye roll.

On the surface, he and I have always been like "every other struggling couple": Our apartment is sparse—decorated with only necessary furniture, our savings account holds less than five hundred dollars, and we've spent more time apart than we have together over the past three years.

That's all part of our promise though. At least it *was*...

While I worked three jobs to put him through law school, he studied all day, every day, and eventually graduated at the top of his class. The day he received an offer from the top law firm in Nashville—three months ago actually, he was supposed to tell me that it was *my turn*. That it was my turn to go to graduate school, my turn to study and pursue my ambitions, while he supported me.

But he didn't.

He didn't say a word about it, and when I mentioned the old promise we'd made, he looked confused. He said that a "real writer doesn't need to go to writing classes," that he'd actually heard a famous writer say those very words. He said the most successful writers "are the ones who write from real life experience and not from what they learn in some classroom."

It took controlling every muscle in my body not to lunge at him, so I resorted to doing the only thing I could do: Cry.

I told him that I understood his thoughts, but I wanted to go to graduate school. I'd already been accepted to Vanderbilt and agreed to go.

His response? Laughter.

"Tell them that your future husband is a *lawyer* now and you don't need them. Law school and writing school are two different things and you know it. One makes money and one doesn't. That's just how it is, but I still believe in your talent. Trust me, things will be much better for us this way."

Much better for us this way...

Everything is always "much better for us this way." *His* way.

"You there, Paris?" He kisses my cheek, bringing me back to the present. "Can we go back to bed now?"

"Yeah." I force a smile and lie down, wondering how long it'll take him to go to sleep.

The second his soft snores begin, I slip out of bed and tiptoe into the bathroom. I look at myself in the mirror and flinch, knowing that the heavy bags under my eyes are from more than working late every day. Frowning, I unclip the photo that's hanging on the wall.

It's always been my favorite picture of us: We're laughing at each other in an onslaught of winter wind, smiling as our hair flies high above our heads. And in the background is the bus stop where we first met.

This is the picture that I always pick up whenever I'm frustrated. It reminds me of the "us" that I remember, the "us" that I loved.

I stare at it for a few more minutes, waiting for that flash of feeling—that "This is just a rough patch, it'll get better" thought that's supposed to click into my mind.

It doesn't.

All I can think about is the fact that we haven't had a two-sided conversation in years. We haven't had sex in forever, and *smiling*? I honestly can't remember the last time I smiled to myself, let alone with him.

I place the picture where it belongs and look into our bedroom, making sure that Adrian is still sleeping. Then I decide to do something that I've dreamed about doing for years: Leave.

I walk over to my closet and grab my largest purse, quietly stuffing it with whatever I can get my hands on. I make sure I have my wallet, my laptop, and my cell phone, and I rush out of our bedroom.

The second I make it into the kitchen, I stop.

I have no idea where I'm going. No idea what I'm doing.

I consider saving my dramatic exit for another day, but my eyes catch the ivory invitation that's hanging on our fridge:

You are cordially invited to the (Shhh! It's a secret!)
engagement party of
Paris Weston
&
Adrian Smith, III.
Cocktails will be served at 6 p.m. sharp,
and the unsuspecting bride-to-be will arrive at 7 p.m.

My blood begins to boil.

That damn engagement party is something I definitely don't want to do—something I *begged* him not to do, but he's done it anyway. And he told me all about the "big secret" weeks ago, telling me that I should, once again, trust him about this: "Just pretend that you don't know anything about it when you walk in, okay? Oh, and make sure you smile really big. The ring is *two carats,* so that practically guarantees a smile from you. Could you also do a little gasp once you actually see the ring? I want all my colleagues to know that you're impressed with my selection."

Enraged, I snatch that stupid paper from behind its magnet and rip it to fucking pieces.

Then I calmly pick up each and every shred and throw them into the trash can. (Adrian is a neat freak...)

Nonetheless, I quickly find my rage again and storm out of the house. I slip into my car and slam my foot onto the gas, driving into the night with no destination in mind...

Four hours later...

I have no idea where I am.

All I know is that my car can't possibly go too much farther. The engine is starting to make a clucking noise, and the wire hanger I've been using to keep my muffler attached is scraping the ground.

Pulling over, I get out of the car and slam the door shut. The engine needs to cool off for a bit, so I walk to the rear and take a seat on the trunk.

With my head in my hands, I consider calling Adrian ahead of time to let him know that I'm not coming tonight, that I'm definitely rejecting his proposal. Then again, I remember that for the past three years he's forgotten to tell me "Happy Birthday."

And not just "forgotten."

He hasn't even had the decency to apologize for leaving me waiting at my favorite restaurant alone. Each time he missed it, he'd say, "Aw. I'm so sorry, babe. It *is* your birthday, huh? Well, Happy Birthday! I didn't get a chance to buy you anything yet, but I have something that'll make you feel much better...I got an A on [insert something I don't give a fuck about here]."

Fuck Adrian...

Before I can turn my phone off, I see that I've missed five calls—all from my boss, so I call him back.

"Paris Weston?" he answers.

"George Nicholson. Are we about to play the name game?"

"Spare me your shit today, Paris. Where the hell are you? We just got a whole new set of sweaters delivered and we need someone to get them ready. There are ties that need to be organized, women's heels that need to be shined, racks of slacks that need to be..."

I listen as he goes on and on, as he reminds me of just how pathetic my life really is.

"Paris!" He snaps. "Do you plan on coming in today? You're already late, so you know you won't get a break. Actually, I'll give you a ten minute one if you stay for a few extra hours. It's the least I can do. But if you pick up my favorite coffee on your way here, I'll make it fifteen. Oh, and get me a bagel, too, with my dry cleaning."

"Fuck you, George." I hang up. I've been wanting to tell him that ever since I started working there, ever since he made me more of a personal assistant than a retail clerk.

George calls my phone again and I hit ignore. I know he wants to get the last word, to say, "No, you're *fired*!" like he told the last quitter, but I refuse to give him the chance.

I lean back against my dusty car and sigh, staring up at the sky. I'd give anything to be far away from here right now.

Anything.

All of a sudden, a plane parts through a cluster of clouds and I start to think about how lucky those passengers are, about how many of them could possibly be running away from a broken dream like me.

Then it hits me.

With no hesitation, I jump off my trunk and wrap the wire hanger around my muffler the best I can. Then I drive towards the airport and park in the extended lot—rushing into the terminal as if I'm about to miss a flight.

"Good morning and welcome to US Airways!" The desk agent smiles as I approach. "Will you be checking any bags today, Miss?"

"No..."

"In that case, I'll need a form of photo identification. Can I have your confirmation number, please?"

"I don't have one." I slide my license across the counter. "Do you have any roundtrip flights for four hundred dollars or less?"

"*What?*" She looks confused.

"Do you have any flights for *four hundred dollars or less?*" I enunciate every word. "I need to disappear and I would like to fly somewhere far away. Can you do that?"

She furrows her brow, but she nods and looks at her screen. "Let me check..."

Typing away on her keyboard, she whispers something into the tiny mic that's tucked into her jacket.

I'm pretty sure I heard her say "potential flight risk passenger heading for security soon," but I shake that thought away.

"How long are you trying to get away, Miss Weston?"

"However long four hundred bucks will cover."

She whispers into her jacket again and then she forces a smile. "We have quite a few roundtrip flights in your price range for anywhere between four to fourteen days. Would you like to go up north or further down south?"

"Whichever is the cheapest."

"Okay, up north then." She types for a few more seconds. "Chicago, Boston, New York, Cleveland, Brunswick, and anywhere in between."

"Boston." I like the way it sounds. "Fourteen days if possible."

"And for fourteen days..." She tilts her head to the side. "Unfortunately, since you're booking this so late, you'll have to have two layovers—one in Atlanta and one in Washington. But, if you want to wait until tomorrow morning—"

"No, thanks. How much is it?"

"Three hundred eighty eight dollars."

I immediately hand over my card.

"Are you sure you don't want me to check that bag, Miss Weston?" She hands me a boarding pass and eyes my oversized purse. "It looks kind of *heavy*..." She whispers into her jacket.

"Why do you keep whispering into your jacket? Do you honestly think I have a—" I almost say the word "bomb" and bite my lip. I'm sure security guards will pop out of nowhere and tackle me to the ground at the mere mention of that word.

"No, thank you." I roll my eyes and head straight for security.

As I hand my documents to the guard, I feel my cell phone buzzing. A text from my older sister:

"Don't forget I'm picking you up around six-ish for dinner! Sister Day! Yay!"

I sigh.

I don't have the heart to tell her that I already know about the engagement party, and that she could've stopped texting me her "Can't wait to spend some quality time with you, sis!" ruse weeks ago.

Instead of ignoring her, I text her back. *"I won't forget..."*

"Ma'am?" A deep voice suddenly says, making me look up.

"Yes?"

"Are you waiting on something to *happen*? Is there a reason you haven't placed that bag on the belt?"

I look over my shoulder and see the desk agent from minutes ago speaking to two security guards, pointing in my direction.

Jesus...

I slide the bag off my shoulder, and before I can set it down, a TSA agent grabs it and takes it over to a table.

Unsurprisingly, when I step through the metal detector, the alarm sounds and announces that I've been selected for a "random" security check.

I lift my arms as a woman waves a wand over my body, as she makes extra passes around my stomach.

"I take it you all are just bored today?" I shake my head. "There are plenty of other suspicious looking passengers for you to harass."

"So, you admit that you look *suspicious*? Send her through the detector again, Rob!" She yells over her shoulder.

I walk through it two more times and watch as my bag is emptied, stuffed, and re-emptied again. Then they finally allow me to head to my gate.

After meandering through the hordes of holiday travelers and boarding the plane, I realize that I'm really doing this.

I'm really leaving him.

Chapter 2

By the time my plane lands, I've realized three things: 1.) I need to hurry up and rewrite my list of resolutions. 2.) Babies should be forever banned from all flights. 3.) Some people think sharing a row means they have to divulge their entire life story to you.

I've learned more about the complexities of shoveling cow dung than I'll ever need to know, thanks to the man who was sitting next to me.

"I hope I didn't bore you too much with my talk, young lady." He smiles as he stands up. "If you're ever in California, remember to visit my ranch. I'll show you how to make the finest manure you've ever seen."

"I will definitely do that..." I wait for him to walk away and look over my shoulder. Several passengers have yet to get off the plane so I'll wait to get up; my next flight won't board for another few hours.

Pulling out my phone, I notice that I have new voice mails. Before I can see who they're from, my best friend David's face flashes across the screen.

"Hey, David."

"*Hey, David?*" He mocks me. "Where are you?"

"Um..." I hesitate.

"*Um?* It's Friday and I'm at Starbucks, ready to listen to a week's worth of 'Fuck Adrian' talk. I practically look forward to this every week."

"What? No you don't!"

"Of course, I don't." He scoffs. "Seriously though, where are you? Are you close by?"

"Is Atlanta considered close by?"

The line is suddenly silent. Then I hear him laughing—laughing hysterically.

"Is that the name of a new restaurant downtown? What street is it on? I'm on my way."

"Atlanta as in *Georgia*, David." My voice cracks a bit.

"What?!"

"I um...I decided to leave Adrian this morning. I don't want to marry him."

"Then you could've just said you *didn't* want to marry him. You didn't have to fly out of the state to make your point." He sighs, and then he gets into his overprotective mode. "How long do you plan to be gone?"

"Two weeks."

"*Two weeks?*" He sounds shocked. "Do you have any money? Did you tell your boss?"

"No...And I kinda told my boss to fuck-off a couple hours ago."

"Should I assume that Adrian has no idea that you're in Atlanta?"

"You should." I can practically picture him shaking his head and crossing his arms. Even though we've been best friends for over a decade, whenever I'm upset he treats me like I'm his little sister. (And he hates Adrian...Always has.)

"Okay...I'll have my secretary wire you a couple thousand. Is Atlanta your final destination?"

"Boston."

"*Boston*, Paris?" He raises his voice. "You don't know anyone in Boston! And you damn sure don't—" He stops. "What do you honestly expect to happen when you come back to Nashville in two weeks? Did you *plan* this runaway trip or did you just wake up this morning and decide to jump on a plane?"

I don't answer.

"Figures." He lets out a long sigh. "I'll make some hotel arrangements and have a driver meet you. Do you plan on calling anyone before tonight's event, or are you going to make them hire a search party?"

"You can tell them I'm not coming at exactly six fifty two."

"Why six fifty two? Wait, you know what? I don't even want to know."

"Fine. Just don't say a word about it until then, okay? Not even to Amy."

"Who is Amy?"

"Your girlfriend."

"From last week." He snorts. "This week it's Rachel. Can I tell *her*?"

"*No!*"

He laughs, and then he clears his throat. "I'm very proud of you, Paris. Glad you finally woke up and saw the fucking light— even though the way you're going about it is the stupidest shit I've ever heard. Now, if only we could find someone who knew how to fuck you right."

I hang up and roll my eyes. Conversations with David always end in sexual innuendos, and whenever we're together, people always assume that we're more than friends.

We're not. Far from it.

Although he's insanely attractive and women cling to him like magnets, in my eyes, he's still the boy who popped my bra straps in middle school.

Maybe he's right, maybe this plan IS stupid...Then again, he critiques porn for a living...

I'm two seconds away from jumping out of my chair and screaming, "Please shut the hell up!" to the arguing couple behind me. They woke me up an hour ago, and I haven't been able to go back to sleep since.

Apparently, the douchebag boyfriend is insisting that she suck up her tears and act happy whenever they land to meet his family. She, on the other hand, hates his parents and is threatening to go home and leave him by himself.

I'm tempted to turn around and tell her to leave his ass, but they start kissing.

Ugh...

"Passengers heading to Washington DC," a voice calls over the intercom, "we are about to begin the boarding process. At this time, I ask that any passengers with disabilities and any passengers traveling with small children make their way to the desk."

Knowing that this process will take forever, I pull a notepad from my purse and start to write my newest resolutions. I want these to be my best ones yet.

I'm not going to promise to go to the gym more often—that never works, and I'm definitely not going to promise to eat healthier foods. McDonald's is my go-to comfort food and I'm never giving that shit up.

This year, I'm focusing on the shit I actually *want*. The shit I've been holding myself back from. Starting with number one: "Dump Adrian's ass."

I write that one down twice, and I almost make it my 'number eleven,' but I don't want to waste such a special honor on him.

"First class passengers may now board the plane..."

I scribble a few more, writing the first few things that come to mind.

Before I can read over it and see if everything is exactly how it should be, my zone is called. My seat is listed as "To Be Determined," so I'm pretty sure that means I'll be sitting in the worst possible spot. Right next to the restroom.

Annoyed, I hand my ticket over to the agent.

"Did you *not* want to sit in first class, Miss Weston?" He raises his eyebrow.

"What? What are you talking about?"

He points at his screen. "You have a first class seat for this flight."

I look at him in absolute shock. I've never flown first class before.

"Is that a yes or would you like to graciously give up your seat to a—"

"*Nope.*" I tell him thank you and anxiously take my spot in the boarding line.

Maybe this runaway trip won't be a complete bust after all...

With just two passengers left in front of me, my phone rings.

It's London. My sister.

"Yes?" I try to sound normal.

"Did you forget about me picking you up today? Where are you?"

"I'm..." I want to tell her the truth, but I know she won't understand.

She's been married to her college sweetheart since she was twenty one and she's the epitome of what it means to be a "fairytale chaser." In fact, when I told her that Adrian wasn't the man I thought he was and that I wanted to break up with him, she cried.

She said, "Prince Charming doesn't always wear his shining armor. He has his faults. You shouldn't break up with him just because things have been rough for a few months. Especially not when years of eternal happiness are right around the corner!"

That was the biggest line of bullshit I'd ever heard, and that was also two years ago...

"I guess I just lost track of time," I say. "Can I meet you?"

"Sure! Meet me at Sweet Falls Country Club, back by the pool, okay? We can eat dinner together! It's going to be so much fun! Just you and me!"

I shake my head at her terrible inability to lie. "I'll see you soon."

She squeals as she ends the call.

Finally stepping onto the plane, I find my row and take the aisle seat—silently hoping that the pilot will forego protocol and take off right away.

Adrian's latest text is going to make me vomit: *"Hey, babe. Remember to look shocked at first, but not too shocked. Save your best face for when you actually SEE the ring...If you need an example, check out this video on YouTube. This woman nails it perfectly. Can you also pick up some beer on your way here, too? Keep it in your sister's trunk. The guys are coming over to celebrate with us later."*

I delete his text and damn near throw my phone down the aisle.

Please hurry the hell up and get this plane into the sky...

More passengers walk past me and I nervously bite my nails. I look at my watch and realize that the main doors are about to close. Since it seems as if everyone scheduled for this flight is already on board, I unbuckle my seatbelt and move to the window seat.

"Strawberries and champagne, Miss?" A flight attendant holds out a tray.

"No, thanks. I don't have any cash on me."

"No, Miss." She laughs. "First class passengers get unlimited refreshments before takeoff and throughout the flight. Since it's a little after the holidays, you can have complimentary champagne as well. The only thing you have to pay for is alcohol."

My eyes widen and I happily take the food away from her, stuffing down everything within seconds.

"Ladies and gentlemen aboard flight number 743, the main flight doors will be closing in sixty seconds," an attendant speaks into a mic. "We now ask that you stow away all portable electronic devices, as the pilot will begin taxi take-off once the doors close."

I let out a sigh of relief and lean back in my chair, slipping a pair of shades over my eyes. I've turned off my phone, and I sincerely hope that Adrian's embarrassment at my absence will be as brutal as he deserves it to be.

Before I can drift into dreams of him getting hit by a bus, a deep voice sounds to my left.

"You're in my seat," it says.

"*Am I?*" I don't look over at him. "Or are you just saying that because you almost missed this flight and want to sit in first class?"

"Excuse me?"

"I've tried sneaking into first class before, but just so you know, it doesn't work. They're going to put you out once they realize you don't belong."

He laughs and settles into the seat next to me. "Very cute."

"Ladies and gentlemen..." The flight attendant begins her safety demonstration. "Please sit back and enjoy the flight."

My heart starts to race as the plane picks up speed on the runway, as it launches into the sky.

I'm crossing my fingers and my toes, hoping that nothing will ruin this moment—that I won't wake up seconds from now and realize that this is all a dream.

"Ladies and gentlemen, you are now permitted to retrieve your personal electronic devices," a voice says over the intercom. "You are also free to move about the cabin."

Thank God! It's definitely not a dream!

With my eyes shut, I reach up and twist the air nozzle above my seat—directing it away from me, but I feel a warm hand grabbing mine.

Annoyed, I use my other hand to slide the shades off my face. I prepare my best scowl and get ready to tell this asshole to keep his hands to his side of the seat, but no words come out.

Oh. My. Fucking. God.

I feel my mouth dropping open and try to close it, but I can't.

The man sitting next to me is utter perfection. Period. He's dressed in a flawlessly tailored black suit with sparkling silver cufflinks, a silk tie that's worth my entire year's salary, and I'm pretty sure his shoes are custom made.

His deep green eyes are currently piercing through mine— gleaming in the light. And his pearly white smile is damn near lethal. As he tilts his head to the side, I notice that his jet black hair is slightly curly, that his full lips are beyond tempting.

"Were you about to say something to me?" He smiles.

"Yes." I manage to regain control of my mouth. "Can you let go of my hand, please?"

"Can you admit that you're in my seat?"

"Would you like it back?"

"No, but I think you can turn the air valve *off* instead of making it blow on me. That's a bit rude, don't you think?"

"Sorry." I switch it off and he lets my hand go.

"Where are you headed?" he asks.

I don't answer. I'm still entranced; I've never seen anyone who looks this good in person.

Okay, this might actually be a dream...

"Are you partially deaf?" He raises his eyebrow and leans forward, talking into my right ear. "Where are you headed?"

"The same place you're headed." I manage.

"You don't look like you're dressed for a Washington winter."

"You know," I say, slowly coming back to my senses, "just because we're sitting next to each other, doesn't mean we have to talk for the entire flight." I point at the magazine in his lap. "I'm sure that *Forbes* is just begging to be read. That fiscal crisis headline looks *fascinating.*"

"I've already read it."

"And your iPod?" I point at the white ear-buds peaking from underneath his coat pocket. "Surely you have something to listen to right now."

"It died on my last flight." He smiles again, temporarily rendering me speechless with his eyes. "I think you and I *should* talk for the entire flight."

I shake my head. I've seen this scenario in one too many *Law and Order* episodes: Girl meets hot stranger. Hot stranger charms girl. Girl starts talking about her life and finds herself revealing personal information. Then hot stranger leads her into a dark alley and strangles her to death. Cue theme music...

"No, thanks." I pull my iPod out of my pocket. "My music is fully charged, so feel free to talk to yourself during this flight, but—"

"You seem tense." He lifts the iPod from my hands. "Why is that?"

"Did you just take my iPod?"

"*I did.*"

"Okay." I roll my eyes and hold out my hand. "I don't know if you're from this country or not, but we consider taking other people's shit *stealing*, so I highly suggest that you give that back before I make a scene."

Still smiling, he tucks my iPod into his jacket. "If you'd like, we can go into the restroom and make a scene *together.*"

"Would either of you like something to drink?" The flight attendant interrupts us with a beverage cart.

Neither of us says a word. We simply stare at one another—him with a devilish look in his eyes, me with an annoyed one.

"I'll have a Sprite." I sigh. "And another glass of champagne, please. Actually, make it two."

"The same," Hot Stranger says. "And two gin and tonics."

She nods and makes our drinks within seconds. She waits for us to pull down our trays, and then she whispers, "Happy New Year" before walking to the next row.

I quickly toss back all of my drinks and regret not asking for more. I have the sudden feeling that this is going to be a long flight. I'm also sure that I'm going to have to put this man in his place before we land.

"I think you need one of these." The sound of his voice makes me look at him again.

"What?"

"You need a drink." He holds it out for me. "A *real* drink."

"No, thanks." I push it away. "I don't trust where that's been."

"*Excuse me?*"

"I didn't stutter. I. Don't. Trust. Where. That's. *Been.*"

"You think I did something to this drink?"

"No, but I've watched enough *Law & Order* to know that you could have."

"Law & *what?*"

"*Law & Order.*" I cross my arms. "It's a TV show, and it deals with people like you. People who are nice to strangers, just so they can satisfy their murder addictions and kill them. "

"I look like a *murderer* to you?" He's smirking.

"No, but since I took my eyes off of you for five seconds, you could've used that time to drug my drink."

"You've only been able to take your eyes off of me for *five seconds?*"

"Were you listening to anything else I said?"

"Not a word." He presses the call button above his seat.

"Yes, sir?" A different flight attendant immediately appears by his side, making a failed attempt to hide her flushed cheeks.

"Can I have two more gin and tonics, please? And could you hand them *directly* to my friend to ensure that I don't slip any drugs into them?"

She nods and scurries away, quickly returning. After she hands them to me, she looks my seat-mate up and down, and murmurs, "*Damn...*"

"Is that better?" He looks at me and offers his hand. "I'm Blake."

"I'm *not interested*, but I appreciate the drinks. I'll pay you back when we land."

"I can't know your name?"

"Yes, if you give me back my iPod."

"I'd rather not." He leans forward and squints at the necklace I'm wearing. It's a bouquet of roses with the letter "P" at the center. Then he gently touches my wrist, where my bracelet of red hearts and an Eiffel Tower charm are dangling. "Is your name *Paris*?"

My eyes widen. "No. Nice try, though."

"If you show me your ticket and that's not your name, I'll give you your iPod and leave you alone for the rest of this flight."

"And if it is?"

"We get to know each other a little better...Is that *not* your name?"

My cheeks turn red and I know it's pointless to lie.

"I thought so. Where are you really headed, *Paris*?"

"Florida."

He raises his eyebrow. "Is that so?"

"Yes. That is very *so*. That's why I'm not dressed for the winter."

"Hmmm." His lips curve into a smile. "I hope you enjoy *Florida* whenever you get there."

"I will. Where are *you* headed?"

"Washington. This is my final flight for the day."

"Interesting." I can't take my eyes off him.

"Are you traveling to Florida to see your boyfriend?"

"To get away from him."

He looks confused. "First-time break up?"

"Hundredth. But this time, it's really over."

"I hope so," he says, and I suddenly realize that his lips are a lot closer to mine than they were seconds ago.

I pull away and clear my throat. "What about you? Are you coming back from seeing your girlfriend?"

"I don't have a girlfriend."

"*Please.* I don't believe that." I roll my eyes.

"Why not?"

Pick up a fucking mirror... "I just don't."

"If I had a girlfriend, I wouldn't be telling you that you have the most fuck-able lips I've ever seen."

"*What*?!" I gasp. "What did you just say?"

"Do you want me to say it a little louder?"

"*No*...But you shouldn't say things like that to strangers."

"You're not a stranger. I'm getting to know you better..." He looks directly into my eyes. "How long were you with your boyfriend?"

"Six years."

"Is it really over?"

I don't hesitate. "Forever."

"If he happened to call you when we landed, would you answer?"

I shake my head. His mouth is moving closer to mine again.

"What if he left a message saying that he missed you? Would you fly right back?"

"No..." My breathing slows as he places his hand on my thigh, as his mouth nearly brushes against mine.

"What city are you headed to again?"

"Boston."

"I thought so," he whispers. "How old are you?"

"Ladies and gentlemen, the pilot has turned on the seatbelt sign..." a voice on the intercom says, immediately breaking us out of our moment.

I lean back in my chair with a racing heart, wondering how the hell this man is having such an effect on me, why the hell I'm *liking* it. My eyes are facing forward, but I can feel him staring at me, feel him still caressing my thigh.

As good as it feels, I have to tell him to stop.

"I didn't give you permission to touch me." I push his hand away and face him.

"Then can I have permission to *touch* you?"

"No. And if you do it again, it'll be called molestation. That's a crime."

"A relatively low misdemeanor with a very lenient punishment."

"You sound like a lawyer."

"I *am* a lawyer." His eyes are gleaming. "You didn't answer my last question."

"Twenty seven and still *not interested*. Do you plan on asking me questions for the entire flight?"

"Will you let me?"

God, his smile is fucking perfect... "No." I need a distraction. Fast. "Can I please have my iPod back? I need to listen to something less-intrusive right now."

He looks at me for a long time—looking as if he wants to ask me something else, but he hands me my iPod. "Enjoy your less intrusive music." He pulls out an e-reader and scrolls across a screen of books.

Sighing, I steal one last glance of him before placing ear buds into my ears. I take my list of resolutions out of my pocket and look over them again.

My New Year's Resolutions

1. *Dump Adrian's ass. For Good.*
2. *Stop thinking about Adrian's ass. For Good.*
3. *Start getting massages at least twice a year... If it's under fifty dollars...*

4. *Do something spontaneous and crazy. Just for the hell of it, something that would scare and excite me at the same time...*
5. *Have passionate, hot sex with someone who isn't Adrian. (Okay, me and Adrian never had passionate, hot sex— Why was I with him again? Why was I—STOP IT...Must finish this list...)*
6. *Meet someone who wants to treat me all the time and not vice versa...*
7. *Write everyday...I'm supposed to be an aspiring journalist, but this list is the first thing I've written in months. MONTHS.*
8. *Have passionate, hot sex...with someone who can give me an ORGASM...*
9. *Start working out...Ha! No. Scratch that...I'll come back to number nine.*
10. *And number ten, too...*
11. *And I still need a number eleven ...*

I look over the list again and again, trying to think of something else to write, but nothing is coming.

Ugh...

"You needed to make *a list* to dump your boyfriend?" Blake looks over my shoulder.

"What the—" I immediately fold the paper and put it away. "You're supposed to be reading!"

"I was, but I became intrigued by what *you* were reading." He pulls one of the ear buds out of my ear. "I only got to number three, but it looked pretty interesting. Can I see the rest?"

"*No.* Definitely not."

"Scared of what I might think?"

"I don't care what you think. I don't even know you."

"You know that I'm attracted to you." He tucks a strand of hair behind my ear. "You know that I think your lips are fuck-able, and you're about to find out that if we were alone on this plane, I'd be fucking you against this seat until you screamed my name."

"*What*?!" My jaw drops. "Did you seriously just say what I think you said?"

"Which part?"

"You know what? I'm going to switch seats now."

"It's a full flight." He smiles. "You're not going anywhere."

We stare at each other without saying another word, and as much as I want to berate him for saying that ridiculous "fucking you against this seat" comment, I can't deny that it turned me on. A lot.

"Would you like to ask me questions?" He finally breaks the silence. "Since I've asked you so many?"

"Nope."

"Why not?"

"Because I'm never going to see you again, and once this flight lands, I'm going to be sure to get the hell away from you as fast as I can."

"Are you *wet* right now? You keep crossing and uncrossing your legs."

"*WHAT*?!"

"Is there a problem, ma'am?" A flight attendant suddenly appears, clearly more fascinated with Blake than me.

"Yes. There is *a problem*." I glare at Blake. "I need to switch seats. Right now."

"I'm sorry, ma'am." Her eyes have yet to lose focus on Blake. "This is a full flight. If I could trade seats with you I would, but it's not allowed. Is that all?"

I roll my eyes. "Yes. That is all."

She lets her eyes linger on him for a few more seconds before walking away.

"Was that really necessary?" Blake looks offended.

"You asked me if I was wet, so yes, it was completely necessary. You asking me that is the equivalent of me asking you if your dick is hard."

"*It is.*"

I look down at his lap and hold back a gasp. "You know, for a lawyer, you're pretty damn dumb when it comes to charge-worthy offenses."

"Asking questions isn't a crime."

"*Sexual harassment* is."

"It's not harassment if the *victim* enjoys it."

I have nothing to say to that. My panties have been wet since he first touched my bracelet; they were soaked the second he told me my lips were fuck-able.

"Since you'd rather talk about *drier* things," he says with a smirk, "why did you and your boyfriend break up?"

"It's a long story."

"We have another hour and you'll never see me again. I'm also a really good listener."

I sigh. It might be good to tell someone else what happened.

My family is "Team Adrian" and they never believe me when I tell them how horrible he is—only David. And I'm pretty sure now that he knows that we're over, he won't want to hear too much more about him.

"I'll tell you," I say, "but you have to promise not to interject with any more of your...Your *comments.*"

"I won't." He looks sincere.

"Okay, well...The first couple years were pretty good—they were exciting and I really liked him, but after we graduated from college, things changed..."

"How so?"

"He became a lot more selfish, and he didn't do little things for me like he used to. No random dates, no telling me I'm pretty just because, nothing."

"I paid his way through law school and he was supposed to pay my way through journalism school once he finished. But instead of doing that, he changed his mind and decided that it didn't make sense for me to go to journalism school...According to him, we needed to focus on building a life together, and he needed to focus on making partner at his firm as quickly as possible so he could make *even more* money. After that, 'if I still wanted to go to pointless writing classes' he said he'd pay for it...My credit is beyond shot right now, so I couldn't get a loan for school if I wanted to, and—" I stop. Saying these words aloud makes my heart ache.

"I'm sorry..."

Shrugging, I lean back in my chair. "It's not your fault," I say. "It's mine..."

All those years. All. Those. *Years.*

I was such a fool.

I'd wake up at the crack of dawn to catch a bus downtown, to wait tables at a premier hotel bistro all morning. Then, with backaches that never seemed to go away, I'd walk eight blocks to a dental office where I filed papers from noon until close. After that—usually around six or seven, I'd take a final bus to a private airport and lug lost luggage across the terminal.

I never complained to Adrian about working those three jobs. I never told him how badly my body ached day after day—partly because I was stupid in love, partly because I knew this was only "temporary."

I knew the second he graduated from law school, the second he landed a job, that he would return the favor and help me pursue my dreams.

I was such a fucking idiot...

Blake hands me his other gin and tonic, and I happily toss it back.

"I would have turned on my filter if you had mentioned it was such a bad break up..." he says.

"So you *do* have a filter?"

"Yes." He pulls the handkerchief from his breast pocket and dabs my eyes with it. "It's just hard to turn off when I see someone I'm highly attracted to."

"I'm sure that happens quite often."

"This is the first time in *years*."

I blush and look away from him, refusing to let myself believe that over the last twenty minutes he's made my body react so easily, that he's had this much of an effect on me at all; I've never felt this type of heated attraction with Adrian. *Ever.*

Now, I honestly want him to get my attention again, to strike up another conversation, but he doesn't.

For the rest of the flight, he leaves me alone.

Chapter 3

"Ma'am? Ma'am?" A flight attendant is tapping me on my shoulder, shaking me out of my sleep. "We need to clear the plane for cleaning."

I sit up, realizing that the plane has long landed and I'm the last one on board.

Unbuckling my seatbelt, I notice a small piece of paper on my thigh. I flip it over and read the small scribbled note:

It was a pleasure meeting you, Paris. Have a safe flight to Boston.

—Blake

I'm not sure why I feel upset that he didn't say goodbye (or wake me up), but I quickly brush away the thought. I have an hour to get to my next gate and I'm determined to be one of the first to board so I can finish my nap.

As I head through the connecting tunnel, I take out my phone and see that there are new voicemails: Five from my mother, two from my sister, and one from Adrian.

I listen to his first: "Seriously, Paris? Are you really that fucking immature to where you can't say no to my face? You needed to go across the country? I told you I was sorry about the grad school thing *months ago* and you're still not over it? Is that what this is about? If it is, that's fucking bullshit. You and I belong together and you know it. This is just another silly misunderstanding and I would really appreciate it if you came back. Call me when you land so I can fly you home and we can talk...Remember that the ring is two carats. I spent a lot of money on it, so I think you should be more grateful...Talk to you soon."

Typical Adrian.

No "I'll do whatever it takes to make things right between us," no "I love you" at the end.

Nothing.

I don't bother listening to the other voicemails. I want to wait until I have some alcohol on standby. Until I can comfortably curse aloud and yell at anyone who dares to tell me that dumping Adrian is a bad move.

Too lazy to pull out my ticket, I look up at the wall of screens ahead and look for my gate.

Dallas, Orlando, Boston...Gate F...Delayed? Great...

I squint my eyes so I can better see the number next to the gate, and a voice comes over the speakers.

"Ladies and gentlemen of Reagan International Airport, due to warnings from the National Weather Advisory Board regarding an incoming snowstorm, all of tonight's flights have been indefinitely grounded. Please check with your airline's respective desk agents for updates regarding rescheduling and for hotel accommodations, if you choose to leave the airport. We sincerely apologize for any inconvenience, but please know that the safety of our passengers is our first and utmost concern."

"What?!" "Are they serious?" "Get the fuck out of here!" "I need to get out of here tonight!"

Angry voices are everywhere, and suddenly everyone is pulling out their phones and relaying the bad news.

Annoyed, I head to the nearest desk agent line and return my mother's call.

"Paris!" She picks up on the first ring. "What the hell is going on with you?"

"What are you talking about?"

"You know *exactly* what I'm talking about!" She clucks her teeth. "Adrian's been telling us how you threw him hints about marriage for a while and he was just waiting to buy the perfect ring. You broke his heart today by pulling what you did. Have you even called him? He looked so broken when David told us where you'd gone, when he said you knew all about the engagement party and chose not to show up. David even *cried* as he told us the story..."

I remind myself to punch David in the face the next time I see him. "I'll call Adrian later. I don't feel like talking to him right now."

"Why are you acting this way, Paris? Adrian is a great catch! He's a *lawyer* now! I'm sure he'll take great care of you, and he loves you!"

Holding back sighs, I try not to groan as she continues to list all the things that are *not* Adrian: Caring, considerate, and generous.

Unbeknownst to her, Adrian only cares about himself and the real reason he wanted to propose to me (in front of all his colleagues, mind you) was because it'll move him up in the rankings at his firm for partner. I'd overheard him talking to one of his associates weeks after he landed the job, saying he'd do whatever it took to make partner in five years: "Even if it means I have to marry Paris earlier than I want to...Even if I'm not ready to commit to her for life."

As far as being *considerate*? That's damn near laughable, along with the word "generous."

Just as she's in the middle of telling me how Adrian understands me like no one else can, the desk agent beckons for me to approach the counter.

"Hold on, mom." I say as I step closer. "I need to ask when my flight to Boston will be rescheduled." I hold the phone against my chest and smile at the agent. "Do you have any idea what time the flight will be rescheduled? Will it definitely be for tomorrow?"

"No clue. Would you like a discount voucher to the Marriott across the street? It's ten percent off and a shuttle can take you there and back."

"No, thanks."

"Okay." She shrugs. "*Next!*"

"I wasn't finished." I shake my head. "I'm not trying to be a pain in the ass, but I'm sure this type of thing happens pretty often here so...When can I expect the flight to be rescheduled?"

"Your guess is as good as mine, ma'am." Her voice is flat. "All I know is that all flights are grounded and you're currently holding up my line. Maybe tomorrow? Maybe next week? They usually call and let you know."

"How can there be a *snowstorm* if there's no snow falling?" I point at the window behind her. "And you all had to know that this storm was coming before today! Are there no weather channels in this part of the country? Do you not have *cable*?"

"*Next!*" She motions for me to get out of the way.

"No, no, no. Wait." I sigh. "I'll take the hotel voucher."

She happily rips a sheet off a pad and hands it to me. "Happy New Year's. Next!"

I move to the other side of the counter and pull my laptop from my bag.

"Are you still there, mom?" I hold the phone up to my ear again.

"Oh, I'm here alright. Where are you, if you're not in Boston right now?""

"Washington DC. There's a storm—supposedly, so they've grounded everything."

"Are you going to sleep in the airport? Did I tell you I saw a story about a nest of roaches in a terminal last week?"

"*Mom...*"

"Actually, you deserve to be crawled on a few times after the way you've handled this whole Adrian thing." She changes her tone. "Do you need me to cover your hotel stay for tonight? David said he wired you money, but it won't be in your account until tomorrow."

"You'd do that for me?"

"Of course." There's sympathy in her voice. "Go ahead and pre-pay for it online. I have my card ready."

I pull up the Marriott's website and type in the dates. The second I click "reserve," the words "SOLD OUT" appear on the screen.

"It's sold out, Mom..."

"Just look up another hotel, hon. They can't all be sold out."

Twenty minutes pass and I realize that they *can* be. They are all, in fact, sold out.

Across from me, a family of five starts to set up camp on the floor. Airport employees are handing out pillows and blankets, and there's an announcement about discounted snacks at all the magazine shops.

"I'm just going to stay here." I wave at a man walking down the aisle, signaling for him to throw me a pillow. "It may give me inspiration to finally write something."

"Are you sure?"

"Yeah, it's not that big of a deal. I'll call you in the morning."

"Wait, Paris. Wait..." She hesitates. "I invited Adrian over to talk. He should be here any minute, so if you want, I can put you on speaker phone and maybe be the mediator between you two. I really think you're going through something, and you're just blaming Adrian for—"

"Goodbye, Mom. I love you." I hang up. I should've known there was a reason she wanted to keep me on the phone. She and I hardly ever talk for more than three minutes.

I grab my things and walk down the aisle, searching for an empty spot. I need to be alone for a while.

For half a second, when my mom had mentioned Adrian wanting to talk, I'd felt a lump crawl up my throat. In the past—whenever Adrian would hurt me or do something selfish, I would let that lump build and build until the tears came. And then I would cry until I couldn't cry anymore.

Not today.

I find an empty bench in front of a window and place my pillow on its edge. Before I can get comfortable, I hear a familiar voice behind me.

"Do you need a place to stay tonight?"

I look over my shoulder and see Blake smiling that flawless smile, looking more perfect now than he did on the plane.

"No, I don't. Thanks for the offer, though." I turn around and fluff my pillow.

"Paris..." Blake walks in front of me and kneels down, grabbing my hand—making my body react against its will, with that one simple touch. "I don't think it's safe for you to stay here overnight."

"Actually, I'm pretty sure it is. Everyone here has had to go through security, so I doubt anyone has a weapon. Plus, there are cameras every few feet. Oh, and since TSA thought I was extremely suspicious hours ago, they're probably watching me right now. I think I'll be fine."

"I don't."

"Who cares?"

"You should stay with me tonight. I don't think you'll get much sleep here."

As if on cue, a woman takes a seat on the bench across from me and rocks her crying newborn.

"Do you not remember what you said to me on the plane, Blake? Do you honestly think what you said should make me comfortable enough to go home with you?"

"Yes."

"Well, it didn't. You saying that my lips were fuck-able—"

"*They are.*"

"And that you would be fucking me against the seat if we were alone didn't inspire any confidence. It told me to run far, far away. And that's what I plan on doing. Now, go away."

He looks into my eyes, giving me a look of complete sincerity. "I only said those things because I honestly thought I would never see you again."

"So, that makes it *okay*?"

"No, and I'm sorry. I didn't mean to offend you at all. I'm not very good at light conversation."

"Clearly!"

"They're closing all the restaurants here, so you'll only be able to buy junk food. The restrooms are going to be crowded at every gate, and it's going to be noisy because there are no enclosed rooms. You shouldn't stay here." He actually looks concerned.

"That was a *very* compelling and persuasive argument, Blake. I can tell your years in law school were well spent. That said—"

"What do I have to say to get you to come home with me?"

"There's nothing you can say. I don't know you, I don't trust you, and I'm also not having sex with you."

"I didn't ask you to have sex with me tonight."

"But you will *in the morning*, if I go home with you, right?"

He blinks.

"Oh my god! No, just *no*."

"I'm not going to ask you to have sex with me, Paris. I'm not even going to ask you to share my bed. You can have the guest suite to yourself."

"Does it have a separate bathroom?"

"It does."

"A door that closes and secures from the inside?"

"Yes." He locks his eyes on mine.

"Is it far away from your room?"

"Very far."

I sit still and look into his beautiful eyes, wanting to say yes, wanting to say "to hell with it" and finally do something spontaneous, but I can't bring myself to do it.

I shake my head and pull my hand away from his. "There's another woman over there who looks like she flew solo. Maybe she'll take you up on your offer."

"This offer is exclusively for you." He takes my hand again.

I can't help but laugh. "You're clearly not catching my hints, so let me help you out: I don't know your last name, I don't know where you live, where you work, what you like to do on the weekends, how you spend your spare time, your phone number, your age, and most importantly, I don't know why you think that I'm *still* going to come home with you."

He slowly lets my hand go. Then he smiles and stands up. "My last name is Taylor. I live on Newbury Lane, house number seven. I work at Taylor and Associates—a law firm I started recently. I work on the weekends, and in my spare time I work even more. My phone number is 555-9870, I'm twenty nine, and I think you're coming home with me because you *want* to— because you're *intrigued*." He picks up my bag and slings it over his shoulder. "Was that everything or do you need to know more?"

Chapter 4

Somehow my brain must have managed to fall out of my skull because I'm currently sitting in the passenger seat of Blake's black Mercedes.

We haven't said a word to one another since he started driving, and I've been keeping watch for the first snowflake. I'm trying my hardest not to think about the fact that after he listed all those facts to me, I couldn't get a single word to come out of my mouth.

Half an hour later, we pull into a picturesque neighborhood that's bordered by a lake. In the darkness, I can make out icy white rails that surround the water and what appears to be a private shopping center on the other side.

Blake slows the car and presses a button on his sun visor, making a three-car garage open. As he pulls inside, I look over at the other two cars: A beautiful grey BMW and a dark green convertible.

"Did you pack pajamas?" He opens my door and clasps my hand.

No... "Of course, I packed pajamas. Why?"

"It doesn't look like you packed much. I was going to offer to order you some with our pizza."

"*Order* me some?"

He nods and leads me into his house, still holding onto my hand. "It's one of the benefits of living in this type of neighborhood. You can order anything, and the stores are accessible after hours."

"How many people stay here?"

"A couple hundred."

"Should I assume that they're all wealthy?"

"Probably." He smiles. "Let me show you to your room. I'll order the pizza afterwards."

As we walk past the living room—a room with a slow burning fireplace and all white furniture, he tells me that he's been living here for about two years. He's supposed to attend monthly meetings with the neighbors and show his face at the huge holiday parties, but he never has the time.

"This is my room." He opens the door to a massive beige room with floor to ceiling windows and a balcony, and I have to prevent my jaw from dropping. I've only seen one other room that was halfway as nice as this, and that was on some reality show I saw last month.

"You can sleep here tonight." He places my bag onto the bed. "The bathroom is behind the door to your right."

"I thought you said I could stay in the *guest suite*."

"I think you'll like this room better."

"Okay, either you're delusional or you don't understand plain English. I told you that I wasn't having sex with you, and I wasn't sharing a room with you. What part of that don't you understand?"

"*I'll* be sleeping in the guest suite tonight." He smiles. "But you're more than welcome to join me if you don't like this room."

I roll my eyes. "This will be fine. Thanks."

"Are you sure? I'm more than willing to fulfill all of your needs."

Silence.

What the hell am I supposed to say to that?

"The pizza usually takes about twenty minutes." He opens a closet and tosses a few blankets onto the bed. "If you need anything else, just let me know." He walks away and closes the door behind him.

As soon as I hear his footsteps trailing down the hallway, I start to look around.

There are a few photos hanging on his walls—mostly ones that feature him and a small brown-haired girl. Her eyes are a stunning green like his, and her smile is just as infectious. I assume that she's his daughter until I notice a small note scribbled at the bottom of one photo: "I love my Uncle Blake!"

How cute...

Curious, I step into his massive walk-in closet. All of his suits and ties are organized by color, and his shoes are perfectly arranged inside clear boxes that bear designer names.

I open all of his dresser drawers in search of something that will prove that he definitely has a girlfriend—a picture, a cami-shirt, an earring, but there's nothing. Only more organized ties, and *condoms*. Lots and lots of condoms.

The last two drawers are stocked full of them, and they all boast "XXL" on their wrappers.

Right...

I head into the bedroom and flop onto the bed—quickly calling David.

"Have I ever told you that you have the worst timing in the world?" He answers with a sigh.

"Have I ever told you that best friends can call each other *whenever they want?*"

"I was about to have sex."

"Well, you must not have been too excited about it because you picked up the phone."

"True." He laughs. "Did you make it to Boston yet? I emailed you a list of things I've scheduled for you to do."

"No. I'm stuck in Washington because the flight was canceled. I just wanted to tell you in case you had someone waiting for me at the airport."

"Thanks. Is that all?"

"That, and I'm going to bash your fucking head in whenever I see you again."

"I take it your mom told you I cried at the party?" He chuckles. "My tears were Oscar-worthy."

"I'm sure they were. I'll call you tomorrow."

"Wait. What aren't you telling me, Paris?"

"*What?*"

"There's something you're not telling me. I can sense it."

"It's nothing."

"Please don't make me guess."

I contemplate hanging up right then and there because if there's anyone who can sense when something is up, it's David. "Okay, okay...I'm spending the night with this guy I met on the plane."

"*This guy* you met on a plane?"

"Are you having problems hearing?"

"What's his name?"

"Blake."

"*And?*" He laughs. "Is that all you know about him?"

"No! I know that he's a lawyer, and he um...Trust me, I asked all the right questions."

"You're attracted to him, aren't you?"

"Of course not!"

"Yes, you are." He's smiling, I know it. "If he was able to talk your suspicious ass into going home with him, you have to be *more* than attracted to him. Don't worry, I'm not judging you. As a matter of fact, I think you should fuck him while you're there."

"*What?*"

"I didn't stutter. You need to be fucked, Paris. Badly."

"*David...*"

"I'm looking out for the both of us. I'd do it, but I don't want you to become addicted to me. Besides, it'd be really nice not to hear you complain about another man's dick anymore, or be forced to listen to you whine about how you only cum three times a year."

"*Seriously?*" I'm going to break his neck *and* bash his skull when I get home.

"If you don't sleep with him, you could at least show him some oral appreciation, don't you think? If I let some stranger chick stay in my house for her benefit, I would at least expect a blow job."

I hang up.

My phone immediately rings and I put it on speaker. "I am not fucking him, David! This is a one night thing and I'm just spending the night. That's it. I might be attracted to him, but that doesn't mean that we're going to have random stranger sex."

"Um..." It's a woman. "Is this Paris Weston?"

I gasp. "No... I mean, yes. May I ask who's calling?"

"This is Missy Turner with US Airways Customer Care. Did I catch you at a bad time?"

"Nope." I change my tone. "Not at all."

"Okay. Well, I'm calling to let you know that your flight from Reagan International Airport to Boston Logan International Airport has been rescheduled for tomorrow morning at ten forty five. We're offering complimentary transportation if you're within ten miles of the airport. Will you need any assistance?"

Yes! Yes! Yes! "No, I'll be alright. Thanks for the call."

"My pleasure, Miss Weston. Have a nice night."

I scroll through the emails on my phone and hit confirm on all the sightseeing events that David sent to me: Spa day, tour of historic downtown, shopping gala, another spa day, and a day at The World of Porn.

Ugh, David...

Picking up my bag, I dump everything I packed onto the bed and quickly realize that I didn't pack shit. No toothbrush, body wash, brush, comb, nothing.

All I have are T-shirts, jeans, an array of mismatching bras and panties, and cotton shorts.

"Paris?" Blake knocks at my door.

"It's open."

He steps inside wearing nothing but a pair of white drawstring pajama pants. "Here you are." He holds out a plate of pizza, but I don't take it.

His body is fucking amazing. On the right side of his perfectly chiseled chest is a black tattoo that swirls and dips down to his six pack abs. At the base of it, right where the ink ends, is a deep V with a small trail of hair that leads to what I'm sure is just as impressive.

"Paris?" He's suddenly cupping my chin in his hands. "Are you okay?"

I nod.

He raises his eyebrow, but he doesn't say anything further. He places my plate on the nightstand and sighs. "I'm not sure how you feel about eating dinner together, but if you want more it's in the kitchen."

"You're not going to force me to eat with you?"

"No, even though I know you want to." He smiles. "You'll come out eventually."

"Yeah, tomorrow when it's time for me to leave. Speaking of which, the airline called and my flight takes off at ten forty five so I should probably leave here around eight, right?"

"Probably so."

"Can you tell me which cab company I should use?"

"None of them. I'll take you."

"No, that's okay. You've done enough by letting me stay here...Do they schedule rides in advance or should I—"

"*Stop.*" He presses his finger against my lips. "I'll take you." He leans close as if he wants to kiss me, as if he's going to, but then he stops. "I'll be in the living room, if you need me. There's extra toothbrushes and toiletries in the bathroom cabinet."

"Always ready for one night stands I see..."

"Excuse me?"

"Nothing."

"What did you say about *one night stands*?"

"Just that you seem really prepared—you know, with your drawers full of condoms and your extra toothbrushes. Being an attractive lawyer clearly nets you all you could ever want."

He stares at me a long time, slowly letting a smile spread across his face. "You went through my drawers?"

"Yes, and you don't need that many condoms..."

"I don't." He gently tugs on a strand of my hair. "But since my last client was a condom manufacturer and I won the case, he gave me a lifetime supply." He leans close again, briefly letting his lips touch mine. "As far as the extra toothbrushes and toiletries go, those are *also* from another manufacturer client. And yes, being an 'attractive lawyer' nets me all I could ever want—except for what I want at this very moment." He kisses my cheek before walking away.

I'm not sure how long I stand in that spot—blinking and wondering why the hell he keeps having this effect on me, but by the time I come back to my senses, I no longer have an appetite.

I force myself to eat at least one slice of pizza, and then I make use of one of the thousands of blue toothbrushes that are stuffed in his cabinets.

I'm stealing at least ten of these before I leave...

Unable to sleep, I slip into the hallway and head into the living room, but I don't see him. Before I can turn around, I feel him standing behind me.

"Those are your *pajamas*?" he whispers against my neck, tugging at the loop of my shorts. "They don't look comfortable."

"Well, they are." I lie. "Were you waiting for me to come out all this time so you could stand behind me and whisper weird shit into my ear, or did I wake you up?"

He moves from behind me without saying a word and clasps my hand. Shaking his head at me, he leads me over to the couch and pulls me down with him.

As he unfolds a blanket, he pulls me close and covers us with it. Then he props a pillow behind my head. "Are you comfortable?"

"Yes."

Ever so smoothly, he dims the lights—allowing the flames in the fireplace to be the brightest spot in the room.

I expect him to try and make a move on me, to hit me with one of his over the top sexual comments, but he doesn't. He simply turns on the TV and leans back against the couch.

"What's in Boston?" he asks without looking at me.

"I'm not sure."

"Are you going there for business, or for *pleasure*?"

The way he says pleasure makes my heart speed up a bit. "Neither...It's just a trip to get away and have some time to myself."

"You don't have any concrete plans?"

"You ask a lot of questions." I look at him. "Do you know that?"

"It's the trait of being a good lawyer."

"A *good* lawyer? There's no such thing."

He lifts his head up. "You have something against lawyers?"

"My ex-boyfriend is a lawyer."

"I'm not your ex-boyfriend." He looks offended.

"Yeah, well. You know what they say. All lawyers are practically scum, the only difference is some fuck you over worse than the others."

"You don't have to keep insulting me to get my attention." He puts his arm around my shoulders. "You've had it ever since I saw you on the plane."

"*What?*"

"You can stop trying to act like you're not intrigued by me." He grins and his eyes light up. "I know you want me."

"What the hell are you talking about? You still think sex is going to happen between us, don't you?" I immediately stand up. "You know what? I knew hanging with you was a bad idea."

"*Sit down.*" He pulls me back onto the couch. "I just wanted some company," he says. "It's been a while since I've talked to anyone outside of my clients and my family, so I thought it would be nice to get to know someone new."

"How sad. I know a therapist, if you need one."

"Okay, Paris." He pulls me close and whispers against my lips, "I need you to stop being so fucking sarcastic. *Right now.* It's not having the effect on me that you think it is, and the next time something smart comes out of your sexy ass mouth, I'm going to show you exactly what that effect really is."

I blush and almost close the gap between us, just so that I can taste his lips, so I can see if kissing him will feel as good as I think it would, but he moves away.

"I don't think so." He smiles. "You shouldn't start things that you can't finish."

I feel my cheeks heating even more and stand up, but he pulls me down again.

"*It's A Wonderful Life?*" he asks.

"What?"

"*It's a Wonderful Life.*" He points at the TV. "Do you want to watch it?"

"Sure..." I say, even though it's hard to pay attention to the movie when his fingers are lightly caressing my shoulders, when I can feel him staring at me.

After several scenes have played, and I've failed to feel his eyes turn away from me, I clear my throat.

"Is there a *problem*?" I keep my eyes glued to the TV.

"No."

"Then stop staring at me."

"I'd rather not." He gently cups my chin and turns my head to face him.

Looking into my eyes, he brushes his thumb against my bottom lip—instantly making me wet.

"Since I need your permission, am I allowed to *kiss* you?" he whispers.

"*No...*"

"Why is that?"

My breath hitches in my throat as he presses his mouth against my neck. "Because..."

"Because *what*? It's just a kiss." He kisses my neck again and looks up at me. "Do I have to give you my whole life story before I get your permission? I can do that, if I need to."

I have no idea what he just said. I can't focus because he's currently running his fingers through my hair and staring into my eyes—giving me that same, lusty smile from earlier today.

"*Paris?*" He leans close so we're lip to lip. "What do I have to do to be able to kiss you?"

"Nothing..."

Within seconds, his lips are on mine and his tongue is slowly slipping into my mouth. His hands are caressing my back and my body is giving in.

I let out a soft moan as one of his hands gently threads through my hair, as he whispers something against my mouth that I don't understand.

Shutting my eyes, I murmur as he continues to thoroughly kiss me—directing my tongue with his, not letting me set the pace.

Before I can kiss him back, and suggest that we just continue doing this for the rest of the night, he pulls away.

"Goodnight, Paris." He kisses my cheek and stands up. "I'll see you in the morning."

"*What?*"

"Goodnight," he repeats. "I'll see you *in the morning.*" And with that he walks away, leaving me wetter than I've ever been after a kiss, and ultimately frustrated.

Maybe I should've suggested sex after all...

I don't bother going back to my room. I bring my legs up on the couch and stretch across the cushions, watching the final frames of the movie before drifting to sleep.

Chapter 5

"It's the start of a new day! It's the start of a new day! It's the—"
I hit dismiss on my cell phone's alarm, groaning when I look at the time. Eight o'clock.

Sitting up, I realize that I'm not in the living room anymore. I'm in Blake's room, tightly tucked underneath a soft blanket.

There's a plate of fruit and a Belgian waffle on my nightstand—along with a glass of orange juice, and behind them is a medium sized box.

Intrigued, I pick it up and quickly unwrap it—laughing once I see what's inside: A white silk slip and a note:

THESE are pajamas... You're too beautiful to sleep in anything else...

I smile and quickly eat the food he's set out before taking another shower.

Today is the day that I'll finally be completely alone and able to think about what I'm going to do with my life. I'm definitely going to have to call David and tell him that nothing happened between me and Blake. And when I'm sure that I have the right words to say, I'll call Adrian.

I put on the same clothes I wore yesterday—silently cursing myself for not making better preparations. I'm about to walk out of the room and look for Blake, but my phone rings. Adrian.

Don't answer it...Don't answer it...

It's the fifth time he's called me since yesterday, and I want to send it directly to voicemail, but I can't help but pick up.

"Hello?"

"Hello, Paris..." His voice is low.

"What's up?"

"What's up?" He scoffs. "I call you over and over and leave a voicemail and all you have to say is, '*What's up?*'"

"Do I need to repeat it?"

"No, I'll tell you what the fuck is up. My *girlfriend* of six years randomly decided to ditch me on the same night that she knew that I was going to propose."

"Aren't proposals supposed to be a *surprise*? Maybe she was disappointed in your approach."

"Come home *now*, Paris. We need to talk."

"We're talking right now."

"Seriously?" He sighs, and then he changes his tone. "Look, I'm so sorry for saying all that stuff to you last month...And I'm sorry for being so selfish about my career, but you've got to understand. What's *two more years*? I'll still pay for you to go to journalism school, it'll just be a little later than we planned. I've made sacrifices for you, too. You know? I chose the cheapest law school so it wouldn't be that big of a burden for you and I graduated early, Paris. *Early.* I could've stayed for another year, but I was thinking about you. Wasn't I?"

"*Adrian*..." My heart is hurting. "Just stop... It's over. I don't want to be with you anymore." I can feel tears welling in my eyes. "I know I should've handled this better, but—"

"You don't really want to do this, Paris." He cuts me off. "I know you better than you know yourself...And I really do appreciate all you've done for me. That's why I want to take this next step in our lives and show you just how much I do. I've talked to one of the partners here and he said he'd be happy to give you a clerk job. It pays twice as much as what you're currently making so...You'd be able to support me in getting my PhD. That'll move me up to partner faster, allow you to have money for yourself, and who knows? By the time I get out of school, you may realize that you don't really want to be a journalist, that you'll be happy being my wife and raising our kids...In fact, most of the wives here at the firm don't have master's degrees, so it may be a bit strange if you had one."

"You are so fucking selfish, Adrian." My voice cracks. "Do you know that?"

"I bought you a two carat ring and I'm *selfish*?"

"I have a flight to catch. Is this all you called to talk to me about?"

"I said I was sorry."

"And I said I was *done*. Anything else?"

He hangs up and I let out a sigh of relief, but I know it's only short-lived. He'll call back like he always does and I'll answer. We'll get into another argument until one of us hangs up, and then we'll repeat this process until I crack and run into his arms again.

Except that last part isn't happening this time...

"Paris?" Blake calls from the other side of my door.

"Yes?"

"We need to leave in ten minutes if you want to make your flight."

I wipe a tear away and open the door. "I'm ready."

I'm sure he can sense that something is wrong, but he doesn't mention it. Instead he walks past me and picks up my bag, motioning for me to follow him out to his car.

We don't speak on the way to the airport. In fact, I barely look his way.

That amazing kiss from last night is long forgotten; all I can think about is Adrian's phone call and the two texts he's sent since: *"I find it so ironic that I'M the selfish one, when you almost depleted our savings account for a random trip to nowhere. Is the real reason for your trip to meet someone else? Is that it? You want to fuck someone else before you marry me?" "I'm sorry for that last text, Paris...I didn't mean that...I understand you wanting a break. Just call me when you're feeling better and aren't as upset..."*

"Paris?" Blake's voice gets my attention and I realize he's holding my door open. "You *are* catching a flight today, right?"

"Right. Sorry." I climb out and take my bag from him. "Um...Thank you so much for letting me—"

He slips an arm around my waist and kisses me, making my knees go weak. "You're welcome."

Holding back a smile, I murmur "thank you" and head inside.

I look over my shoulder to get one last look at him, but I realize that he hasn't gotten back into his car. He's following me.

"What do you think you're doing, Blake?"

"I'm making sure you get there safely."

"There's really no need for that. I think I'm perfectly capable of getting on a plane myself. There aren't too many ways that I can fuck that up."

He crosses his arms and I know this is a lost argument, so I ignore his presence and walk up to a desk agent.

"How may I help you today, Miss?" She looks up.

"I'm here for my rescheduled flight to Boston." I slide my license across the desk. "Paris Weston. Would it be possible to have a window seat?"

"I'm sorry, ma'am. That flight was canceled fifteen minutes ago."

"*Fifteen minutes ago?*"

She nods. "You should be receiving a phone call or a text notification any minute now."

As if on cue, my phone vibrates and I hold it up to my face. It's a text: "*This is a message for all passengers who have flights booked out of Reagan International for the next five days. All flights have been indefinitely grounded due to concerns from the National Weather Board regarding the snow storm that is set to move to the area over the next week. Please check with your specific airline regarding refunds, rescheduling, and hotel affiliate reservations.*"

"Five days?" I glare at her. "Are you fucking kidding me?"

"Ma'am..."

"No, are you *fucking kidding me?*" I notice a security guard walking over, and lower my voice. "I'll still have seven days left after the weather passes, right? Can you book me on the next available flight, please?"

"Did you purchase flight protection?"

"No."

"Well, in that case...It'll depend on the number of passengers that are already scheduled for that flight and open availability. Customers with flight protection will receive the first tickets."

I try to stay calm. "Well, can I fly somewhere else then? Somewhere that costs the same amount?"

"All US Airways tickets are nontransferable, Miss Weston. Would you like a refund for that portion of the trip?"

"Are you saying that I'm *stuck* here?"

"I didn't personally say that but...Given the number of stranded passengers and the fact that you didn't buy flight protection..." Her voice trails off. "Your return flight to Nashville won't be affected at all. In fact," she says, tapping on her keyboard, "I changed it so you won't have a layover in Atlanta this time. It's a direct flight now. Would you like a refund for the Boston portion of your trip?"

"No, I would not like a fucking *refund*. I would like for you to—"

"She'll take the refund." Blake covers my mouth with his hand and gives me a look of sympathy.

I bite my tongue, preventing myself from telling him to stay out of this.

"Here you are, Miss Weston." The agent hands over a voucher. "I also refunded your first flight in light of the circumstances. I really am sorry for the inconvenience." She has the decency to look halfway sincere.

"Thanks." I sigh and let Blake lead me out to his car. There's not a single fucking snowflake falling from the sky and I'm tempted to run inside and demand to speak to the CEO.

"Are you really that upset about missing your flight?" Blake speeds onto the highway.

"Of course I'm not upset. I buy flight tickets with no intention of flying all the time."

"I meant to imply if you were upset about spending more time with *me*."

My eyes widen as far as they can go. "*Excuse me?*"

"You're more than welcome to stay with me until after the storm passes."

I burst into laughter. He's out of his mind.

"Is my hospitality that funny?"

"It is." I take a deep breath. "No offense, but I don't really trust you."

"You could, if you wanted to." He smiles. "Stay with me."

"No, thanks." I shake my head. "I mean, we were only together for a few hours yesterday and you were assaulting me with your tongue, so I can only imagine what you would attempt to do with even more days."

"I *assaulted* you?"

"That's what I said."

"I don't recall you asking me to stop." He looks over at me. "As a matter of fact, you looked disappointed when I did. And if I was sensing things correctly, I think you wanted me to take things further—*a lot* further."

My cheeks redden and I focus my attention on the buildings that are whirring past my window. Staying with Blake for over a week would definitely be the most spontaneous thing I've ever done in my life, but I can't bring myself to admit that out loud.

"Can you take me over there, please?" I point at the hotel park that's up ahead. "I'm going to get a hotel room."

"I'm pretty sure they're sold out already."

"I'm pretty sure you want me to believe that."

He laughs and pulls off onto the next exit ramp. Instead of heading straight for the park, he coasts into a Starbucks drive thru.

"I have a feeling that this is going to be a very long and eye-opening day for you," he says. "Would you like anything to drink?"

"Caramel Frappuccino..." I hold out my credit card, but he doesn't take it.

"My pleasure."

After handing me my coffee, he turns to face me. "I won't attempt to do anything you don't want to do, Paris. I'm just being nice and trying to save you some money. And I wasn't joking about needing new company. *Stay with me.*" He brushes a hand against my cheek.

"Um..." *Say yes...Hell fucking yes...* "Can we stop at the Marriott first?"

He rolls his eyes and drives over, parking at the mid-point for all the hotels.

"Thank you." I immediately jump out of the car, but I feel him walking by my side seconds later.

We step into the first hotel—a midscale type of place with glass elevators and a sparkling lobby, and I notice that everything seems quiet. Empty.

Before I can tell Blake, "Told you so," I see a sign hanging a few feet above the front desk: *"Sorry, We're Sold Out."*

I frown and leave, walking next door to another hotel.

Sold out.

Then another.

Sold out.

By the time I reach the eighth one, my patience is wearing thin and the permanent smirk on Blake's face is driving me insane.

"Shall we go to the next one?" He holds a door open for me. "Or have you given up yet?"

"I'm not giving up..."

"Because you're scared to stay with me, or because you actually don't want to give up?"

I pretend as if I didn't hear that question. I'm sure the loud beating of my heart answered it for me.

The next hotel we enter is relatively small and quaint, and I expect to see a sold out sign on the desk, but there isn't one. The lobby is relatively bare and the carpets could use a serious cleaning, but it looks good enough.

"Good afternoon and welcome to Eco-Suites." A man with a scruffy beard appears behind the desk. "How may I help you two?"

"It's just for one." I look over my shoulder and see Blake talking on his cell phone. "I need a room until next Sunday, please."

"Next Sunday?" He types on his keyboard. "I can do that for eighty three dollars a night—cash, ninety nine if you're using a credit card."

"Sounds great." I pull out my wallet.

"Oh and by state law," he says, lowering his voice, "I'm required to tell you that we're in the middle of renovating our rooms."

"Okay...Why would that be a problem?"

"It's not. Most people just like to know whenever there's a bed-bug outbreak." He shrugs. "It's not that big of a deal in my opinion."

"I'm sorry, *what*?" I freeze. "Are you *renovating*, or are you *fumigating*?"

"*Fumigating*," he repeats. "That's the word I was looking for. Same thing."

"Are you out of your damn mind? It is not the same thing!"

"So, you don't want the room anymore? What about for fifty a night? That's as low as I'm allowed to go."

I take a deep breath. "No, thanks." I turn around and look at Blake who is now giving me an 'I told you so' look.

"There's another hotel park two miles down," he says. "I can take you there as well, if you'd like."

I don't say anything in response. I follow him back to his car, and he unlocks the door—stepping in front of me before I can get in.

"Am I taking you to the other hotel park or have you finally come to your senses?"

"You're taking me to the other hotel park." I mutter, but I quickly change my answer. "I'll take you up on your hospitality offer, but only under two conditions."

"And what conditions are those?"

"Number one, you can't kiss me again." I try not to smile. "*Seriously*. And number two, if I get drunk, which I probably will, given the circumstances, you can't take advantage of me."

He steps out of the way—motioning for me to slip inside.

"*So?*" I refuse to get into his car until he agrees. "What do you say? Do you agree to those conditions?"

"Not at all."

"What? Why not?"

"Because I am going to kiss you again." He leans close. "Seriously. And you won't be drunk when you beg me to take advantage of you. You'll be completely sober." He tucks a strand of hair behind my ear, making my heart race ten times faster. "Those are *my* conditions. Can you agree to those?"

I look away from him and slip into the car—hoping I won't regret checking off my number four.

Chapter 6

"Is that everything?" I place a shopping bag onto the kitchen counter. "Can I go to my room now?"

"No." Blake smiles and leads me into the living room, motioning for me to lean back against the pillows. For the past few hours, I've been tagging along and watching him shop for storm supplies.

Even though I thought the people in this city were overreacting to this invisible storm, the second we finished buying fleece blankets, the parking lot had been covered in a light snow and the skies had turned grey.

"It'll probably get worse as the days go on," he'd said. "We should probably get a few more things."

Those "few more things" turned into a lot more things, and I swear we stopped at every store in sight. He bought candles, flashlights, sleeping bags, draft sealant, and, to "thank me for being his company," he bought me four silk slips and a white robe. As ridiculous as some of the comments he made were ("You should model those slips for me one night..."), I actually enjoyed being around him.

"Are you tired?" He turns on the fireplace.

"No, just disappointed."

"Why?"

I shake my head. I don't want to bore him with anymore talk of Adrian.

"Why, Paris?" He walks over to me and raises his eyebrow.

When I don't say anything, he sits on the couch and pulls me into his lap. Before I can move, he begins to massage my shoulders.

"Are you *from* Nashville, Paris?" he whispers.

"Born and raised...You're from DC?"

"Seattle."

"You took a flight from Seattle to Atlanta and then to DC? That doesn't make any sense."

"I didn't create the flight plan." His hands softly rub the back of my neck. "But I'll be sure to share your concerns with the airline the next time I fly."

"You should..." I bite my tongue so I won't murmur, so I won't give him any idea about how good his hands feel. "You should definitely do that...Next time you fly..."

"Tell me why you're disappointed."

I say nothing, and he gently tilts my head back until I'm looking into his eyes.

"Tell me."

"I don't want to hate my ex-boyfriend anymore."

"Then *don't.*"

"Easier said than done..." I sigh as he caresses my shoulders again, as he blows soft and gentle kisses against my neck.

"Can I ask you something?"

"I am not wet. Does that answer it?"

"No, but that's *a lie.*" He trails a finger down my spine. "That also isn't what I was going to ask you."

I cross my legs and he laughs.

"Why did you have to pay to put your boyfriend through law school in the first place?"

"Because we regular people don't have rich parents that can afford to pay for school. It was a trade-off. Since he was going to have the more lucrative career, we agreed that he needed to finish school first."

"I worked my way through law school. My parents didn't pay for anything."

"Oh, I'm sorry. I just thought that..." I pause. "I'm sorry for assuming."

He runs his fingers through my hair. "Since you broke up, is he going to pay you back for his tuition?"

I burst into laughter, nearly falling out of his lap. *"Pay me back? Is that a joke?"*

"It only seems fair."

Fair? Ha!

I wipe my eyes on my sleeve, still laughing. I can't imagine Adrian paying me back for anything. As a matter of fact, if there was a way that he could sue me for not accepting his engagement ring, I was sure that he would try.

"My boyfriend—*ex* boyfriend, I mean, has always seen everything in black and white. I'm pretty sure he thinks that I voided our deal by leaving him, so he technically doesn't owe me anything."

"That's unfortunate." He stops touching me and hesitates. "Were you in love with him?"

"For the first two years, yes," I say. "But after we moved in together, I slowly fell out. I just didn't want to believe it was happening."

I remember how I practically coerced Adrian into saying that he "still loved [me]" years ago, that he probably only said it so I would continue paying for his studies.

"What about you, Blake?" I quickly change the subject.

"What about me?"

"Since you claim you don't currently have a girlfriend, I'm sure you have a long-lost-ex sob story."

"I don't."

"Right..." I roll my eyes. "If the way that flight attendant reacted to you was any indication, I'm sure women fawn over you all the time."

"They do."

"So, you *are* a one-night stand type of guy? You sleep with every woman who flirts with you? Reel them in and dazzle them with your life's supply of condoms?"

"If that was true, I'd be sleeping with you." He kisses the back of my shoulder before standing up. "I sacrificed a social life for the firm's startup. I didn't need any distractions." He tilts my chin up. "Though I must admit, if I had met you sooner, I might have made an exception."

I uncross my legs, earning another low laugh from him.

"I'll be right back," he says, and I look away. I need to figure out a way to get to my room and stay there for the rest of this trip. If I don't, I'm pretty sure he'll be having his way with me all over the house.

"Are you a fan of shots?" Blake suddenly steps in front of me, holding a tray of red colored shot glasses.

"What type of shots?"

"Vodka, but these are drinking game shots."

"We can't just drink without playing some type of game?"

"We could." He sits next to me and sets the tray on the coffee table. "But since you've said that we don't know each other that well, I think this is a good way to start." He reaches out, drags a finger against my lips. "Do you know how to play *Never Have I Ever*?"

No... "Yes." I feel him caressing my cheek with his other hand.

He must sense that I have no idea what that game entails, because he begins to explain. "I'll say something, something like 'Never have I ever sat next to a beautiful stranger on a plane.' Since that's true, I'll toss back a shot. You will, too." He laughs. "Then it'll be your turn to tell me something you have or *haven't* done before..."

My cheeks are on fire.

This is a bad idea. A very, very bad idea.

"Umm..." I notice him moving closer to me. "I'm not sure if we should play a game like that. Can we just watch another movie?"

"No."

"*No?*"

"No." He hands me a shot. "You're too much of a distraction for me to focus on a movie. It barely worked the first night."

"You're forcing me to play?"

"Yes. Are you ready?" He grabs a drink for himself. "We can start things off simple. I'll go first: Never have I ever kissed a stranger."

We both toss our drinks back and I quickly grab another.

"Um..." I search for something to say. "Never have I ever...kissed someone in a car."

He raises his eyebrow as he tosses a drink back. I consider tossing mine back so I won't seem lame, but I don't want to take any unnecessary shots.

"You dated your boyfriend for *six years* and he never kissed you in his car?"

"He wasn't into public displays of affection." I shrug. "Neither was I, honestly. It wasn't our thing."

"Hmmm..." He picks up another shot. "Never have I ever slept naked."

We both toss drinks back.

"Never have I ever..." I laugh. "Never have I ever sat on a couch with someone who I once thought was a murderer."

"*How creative...*" He rolls his eyes and I down my drink.

"Your turn," I say playfully. "Why don't you say something like, never have I ever harassed a woman on a plane?"

"No, thank you." He looks directly into my eyes. "Never have I ever wanted to sleep with a stranger. A *beautiful* stranger."

"Sleep with? You mean like cuddle?"

"I mean like *fuck*." He picks up a shot and slowly pours it into his mouth, seemingly waiting for me to do the same, but I don't make a move.

"How revealing of you, Blake. That's very interesting, and also very *sad*... Never have I ever—"

"The purpose of this game is to tell the truth." He cuts me off.

"Okay. *And*?"

"And if someone isn't telling the truth," he says as he grips my hips and pulls me into his lap—letting me straddle him, "they can be challenged and made to drink an extra shot."

"How scary." I can feel his dick hardening underneath me. "Please, tell me more."

He rubs his hands up and down my sides. "The thought of sleeping with me hasn't crossed your mind?"

"Nope."

"Is that honestly true?"

"Is there another type of *true*?" I try to move out of his lap, but his grip is too tight.

"You weren't dreaming about me fucking you last night? After I kissed you, you didn't want more?"

"How many different ways do you plan on asking the same question?" I keep my voice firm. "I said that I've never wanted to sleep with a stranger—that includes you. That means that I haven't dreamed of fucking a stranger—that *also* includes you. Also, while we're on the topic of—" I stop.

His hand is sliding into my jeans, stopping right at the crotch of my panties. He's tapping his finger against the soaked spot, narrowing his eyes at me as he does it.

"You were saying?" He raises his eyebrow.

"I was saying that..." I gasp as he pushes my panties to the side and slips a finger inside of me. "I was saying that..."

"That you've *never* wanted to sleep with me?" he whispers. "That you *weren't* wet when I massaged you?"

"Yes."

He slips two fingers inside of me and moves them both in and out, keeping his eyes locked on mine. "There are penalties for lying in this game."

"So?" I barely manage; his thumb is gently circling my clit.

"So, I'm going to give you a chance to change your answer." He kisses my neck. "Are you sure that you've never, *ever*, wanted to sleep with me?"

"Absolutely." I suck in a breath as his fingers slide deeper and deeper.

"How sure?"

"Very..." I'm breathless. "Ten hundred percent sure, to be exact."

He smiles and slowly pulls his fingers out of me, then he brings them to his mouth and licks them clean.

OH. MY. GOD...

My mouth is hanging open. I'm not sure if he really just did that.

"*I did,*" he says, as if he can read my mind. Then he reaches into his pocket and pulls out a crumpled sheet of paper. "My New Year's Resolutions...Number five: Have hot and passionate sex with someone who isn't Adrian..."

I can feel all the color leaving my face, feel my heart pounding louder and louder. "Where did you get that?"

"It fell out of your jacket this morning when I took you to the airport. I was actually about to toss it away and drive off, but once I opened it and read it, I decided that wasn't the best idea..."

"So what?" I shrug and regain my composure. "That doesn't mean that I wanted to have hot and passionate sex with *you*. I didn't even know you when I wrote that list."

"Number eight." He looks at the paper again. "Have hot and passionate sex...With an ORGASM..."

"Once again, there's no mention of you, so—"

"Right underneath that, in a different colored pen, you added 'someone like Blake, maybe?' in very small print. Would you like to see that part for yourself?"

I gasp and snatch the paper away.

"I'm more than happy to help you check off both of those numbers." He leans forward and whispers, "All you have to do is tell me that you want me..."

Mortified, I suck in a breath and jump up. "I'm done playing this game."

"I'd feel the same way, if I was losing." He smiles. "Are you going to congratulate me on my win or are you going to be a sore loser and leave me all alone?"

"Fuck you, Blake."

"I'd love for you to."

I roll my eyes and head down the hallway to "my" room. I double lock the doors again and again, and as soon as I'm sure that they're secure, I fall back onto the bed.

I can't believe he found my list, that he knew that I wanted to sleep with him all day and kept any mention of it inside.

I hold the paper up and notice that he's written notes next to a few of my resolutions:

3. Start getting massages at least twice a year... If it's under fifty dollars...

(I'd be more than happy to give you as many of these as you like...)

4. Do something spontaneous and crazy. Just for the hell of it, something that would scare and excite me at the same time...

(We should discuss this...)

5. Have passionate, hot sex with someone who isn't Adrian. (Okay, me and Adrian never had hot, passionate sex—Why was I with him again? Why was I—STOP IT...Must finish this list...)

(I'm not sure why you were with him either, but I would love to help you satisfy this resolution...)

6. Meet someone who wants to treat me all the time and not vice versa...

(Let me take you on a date after the storm is over...)

7. *Write everyday...I'm supposed to be an aspiring journalist, but this list is the first thing I've written in months. MONTHS.*

(I have a private library you can use.)

8. *Have passionate, hot sex...with someone who can give me an ORGASM...*

(Multiple.)

Chapter 7

There's a heavy snow falling outside my window. It's blanketing everything in sight, and under the night's grey skies, the scene looks surreal.

I want to step outside on the balcony and toss my phone into the snowflakes, but I can't seem to stop listening to Adrian's latest speech.

"Please stop calling me, Adrian," I say. "I took a flight to get away from you for *a reason*."

"Tell me where you are, so I can drive to you...It doesn't matter how far." He actually sounds sincere. "Please."

"No, thank you."

"Paris, I'm sorry. I really want us to work this out."

"What's the point, Adrian? Do you even love me anymore? Did you ever?"

"What type of question is that? Of course, I loved you. I still do."

"That's why you want to marry me?" Tears have been falling down my face ever since I stupidly picked up the phone.

"Yes, Paris. That's exactly why. I want to spend the rest of my life with you."

"So if I say no, if I say that I think we should wait a few years...What would you say to that?"

He hesitates. "Why would you say *no*?"

"Answer the question."

"Babe...Seriously, where are you? We need to discuss this in person."

"We can discuss it right now." I wipe my face on my sleeve. "You still haven't answered my question."

"If you said no..." There's a bit of anger in his voice. "I guess I would just let you say no...But I would also say that it would probably be easier for us, if we got married."

"*Easier?*"

"Financially easier. I'll make partner a lot sooner if we're married, and I'll be able to send you to whatever writing school you want. Well, after I go back to get my PhD, but that's only a few more years."

"Goodbye, Adrian." I end the call and turn off my phone.

More tears stream down my face and I check the time: Three o'clock in the morning. I know that I shouldn't have picked up, but a small, foolish part of me honestly thought that he would beg to have me back, that he would finally act like the man I wanted him to be.

I turn on the lamp and pull out my list—looking at number two, "Stop thinking about [him]," and place a large checkmark by it.

I won't be answering his phone calls anymore.

"Paris?" Blake's voice is in my ear. "Is something wrong? Are you sick?"

I murmur and roll over to face him.

The second I open my eyes, I almost fall out of the bed.

He's damn near naked. He's only wearing a towel around his waist, and small droplets of water are trickling down his tattooed chest. To make matters worse, the imprint of his dick—his HUGE dick, can clearly be seen through the towel.

Holy shit...

"Paris?" He places his hand on my forehead.

"Why the hell are you *naked*?" I'm sure my eyes are as wide as they can go.

"You were screaming."

"I screamed for you to come in here and take your clothes off?"

"No." He laughs. "I heard you while I was in the shower... Are you listening to me?"

I try to keep my eyes on his, but they keep wandering down to that towel—attempting to get a better look at exactly what's behind it.

"Would you like for me to take the towel *off*?" he asks. "I'm starting to think that would really make you feel better."

"It wouldn't." My heart flutters. "And I'm perfectly fine. I think I might have just been moaning about menstrual cramps."

"I highly doubt that."

"Because they taught you how to predict menstrual cycles in law school?"

"No, but you took a birth control pill while we were on the plane—a first week Thursday one...You won't get your period for another *two weeks*, so I highly doubt you're having menstrual cramps—if you're even cramping at all."

My jaw drops and the fluttering in my stomach intensifies.

He smiles at me, damn well knowing that he won that last conversation. "Did you want to sleep the rest of the day away, or do you want to join me for dinner?"

"Depends. Do you want to put some actual clothes on?"

"If you insist." He helps me up and walks me into his dining room.

After he pulls a chair out for me, he disappears for a few minutes and returns in grey flannel pants. He places a plate of grilled chicken and rice in front of me, and pours me a glass of red wine.

I avoid eye contact as I eat—trying not to murmur with each and every bite.

God, he's an amazing cook...

"Paris?" He calls my name, but I don't look at him.

"Yes?"

"Can I ask you something? It may be slightly invasive..."

"I don't think you're capable of being anything but *invasive.*"

"If the sex wasn't as good as you wanted it to be with your boyfriend, why didn't you ever tell him how you felt?"

I immediately look up. "Why would I do that?"

"Why *wouldn't* you?"

I lean back in my chair, thinking.

The first time Adrian and I had sex, we were at a luxury hotel downtown and he'd paid for us to have the room all weekend.

He was the third guy I'd been with, and I was just grateful that he wasn't being rough and rushing through it like my last "kind of" boyfriends had. He'd kissed me gently all over, whispered sexy things into my ear, and when he'd slid into me it felt nice.

Just nice.

The times after that—for the first two years that we were together anyway, the sex was good, but it gradually became all too similar. Slow. Gentle. *Calculated.*

No matter how frantic and heavy the foreplay was, the actual sex was never spur of the moment, never "right here, right now," never interesting. In fact, I could practically predict how many times he would kiss me before and after, could practically predict all the words he would say: "You're amazing, Paris..." "Is this good?" "Keep going, Paris..."

Still, it was never "bad sex," just "nice sex."

"We didn't really talk about sex," I say, avoiding Blake's eyes. "We just did it. And honestly, it wasn't terrible. It just wasn't—"

"Hot and sweaty?"

"*Passionate.*" I correct him. "After our third year together, we were both working so hard that sex kind of faded into the background. We were working like crazy, and staying on top of everything was way more important than a romp in the sheets...Besides, sex can always get better with someone you love. You don't dump someone just because it's not 'out of this world.' You just work on it together."

He doesn't say anything. He just stares at me with a blank expression.

"You'd dump your girlfriend if the sex wasn't good?" I scoff.

"I've never had a girlfriend."

WHAT?! "Who's lying now?"

"It's the truth. I've never had one."

Unbelievable... "Next thing you'll tell me is that you're a virgin."

He blinks.

"Wait, wait, wait..." My eyes widen. "*Are you?* Are you a virgin?"

"A what?"

"A *virgin*." I stare at him in shock. "That would actually explain a lot...*A whole lot.*"

"Would it really?" He stands up and walks over to me, leaning against the edge of the table.

"It would...You really are a virgin, aren't you?"

"Care to share how you could ever come to that conclusion?"

"Simple really." I replay the past few days in my mind and realize that it really does make sense. He could really be a virgin "Well first of all, you flirted with me a lot on the plane and you said some outrageous sexual shit, but you admitted that you only did that because you thought you'd never see me again. Because you knew you'd never have to prove it, because you couldn't due to your lack of experience."

He raises his eyebrow, but I continue.

"The other night, when you asked me for a kiss, you just kissed me and that was it. No *non-virgin* would do something like that. He would at least try to take things a little further, try to touch me somewhere else." This is all adding up and I almost feel silly for not picking up on this sooner. "And then last night, when we were in the middle of playing Never Have I Ever, you tried to make it seem like you were sooo good at sex. Typical virgin behavior. And you finger-fucked me. Seriously? I haven't been finger fucked since I was in tenth grade...Oh, and it was by a guy who was *also* a virgin."

"Are those all of your reasons?" He leans closer and blows a strand of hair away from my face.

"You need more? Everything I've said is pretty concrete." I cross my arms. "Oh, and add in the fact that you've *never* had a girlfriend. That's a dead-ass give away...You know what else? I'm pretty sure you have a porn collection buried underneath your lifetime supply of condoms. So if you'd like, we can watch a video together and I can explain sex to you. I can tell you all about it."

He's silent for a long time, simply looking at me—letting me know that I'm completely right about his virgin status. Then he suddenly grips me by my hips and lifts me up, setting me on top of the table.

He slides his fingers against the sash of my robe, slowly pulling it open.

"Let's get a few things straight, *Paris*." He sits in the chair I was sitting in, positioning himself right between my legs. "I haven't been a *virgin* since I was fifteen years old."

My cheeks immediately turn red.

He opens my robe a little more. "I *have* flirted with you a lot this weekend and changed the subject quickly after I said something sexual, but only because if I actually told you *how much* I wanted to fuck you, you might've never come out of your room."

I gasp as he slides a hand up my bare thigh.

"*The other night*," he says, mocking me, "when I asked you for a kiss and that was it...I *did* want to take things further and touch you somewhere else. But I didn't want you to feel like I was taking advantage of you."

He leans forward and places his hands on my shoulders, slowly pushing my robe down my body—exposing the fact that I'm wearing nothing but a bra and panties underneath. "And last night, during Never Have I Ever, I wasn't trying to make it *seem* like I was "sooo good at sex." I *am* good at it—very, *very* good at it. And the only reason I slipped my fingers inside of you, was because I thought you would run off if you felt my dick."

I am utterly speechless.

And I can't move. I'm frozen to this spot on the table, unable to control my body's reaction to him anymore.

"What was that last reason you gave that made you think I'm a *virgin?*" He presses a kiss against my stomach.

"You..." I murmur as he pulls my panties down to my ankles. "You've never had a girlfriend..."

"*Right.*" He blows a kiss against my thigh. "I've never had a girlfriend because I've never had the time."

"I didn't mean to offend you..."

"No need to apologize." He spreads my legs even further. "For the record, I don't have a porn collection. But if I did, I think *I* would be the one explaining sex to *you.* Don't you think?"

My heart nearly jumps out of my chest, but before it can, Blake grips me even tighter. "Lie down."

"Um...I'm not sure if—" I don't get a chance to finish that sentence. The next thing I know, my back is being pressed against the table and Blake is kissing my neck.

Trailing soft kisses down to my stomach, he slides his hands underneath my thighs and pulls me closer to his mouth, softly blowing against my clit.

"Whoa, wait." I immediately sit up. "Are you about to—"

"Fuck your pussy with my mouth. Is there a *problem?*"

"No...but—"

He presses his finger against my mouth and pushes me back against the table. Before I can take another breath, I feel his lips sucking on my clit, feel two of his fingers plunging deep inside of me.

"*Ahhh...*" I reach down and thread my fingers through his hair. "*Fuck...*"

I shut my eyes as his tongue swirls around my lips, as he whispers, "You taste so fucking good..."

As he starts to flick his tongue against me harder, I try to push his head away—to get him to slow down, but he doesn't. He grips my thighs tighter, and slips his tongue inside of me even further.

I expect him to stop any minute now, for him to take a break, but he never breaks his rhythm; he never slows for a single second.

"*Blake...*" My legs are quivering and I can't control my breathing. "*Blake...*"

Not answering me, he lifts one of my legs up and places it over his shoulder.

"*Blake....Blake, stop...*"

He squeezes my ass and continues to fuck me with his tongue, attacking my clit with kisses that make me scream his name louder and louder.

With my eyes still shut, I try to grab his head one last time and push him away, but he takes my hand and holds it still. Just as I'm about to yank it free, my body starts to convulse.

Tremors travel up and down my spine, and I feel myself getting closer and closer to an orgasm.

I feel Blake leaning over me and kissing my neck, whispering, "Let go, Paris," and I scream—letting waves of pleasure roll through me over and over again.

My hips continue to shake as I open my eyes, and Blake rubs his palms against my thighs until they stop.

I lie there, panting, for what feels like forever—unsure of what the hell just happened. I mean, I've had that done to me before but not like that. *Never* like that.

Jesus...

Blake closes my legs and slips an arm underneath my hips, slowly lifting me up.

He re-fastens my robe without saying a word, and then he looks into my eyes. "I'm going to finish my shower. I'll meet you in the living room in a little bit. Maybe you can think of another game we can play?" He trails his fingers against my lips before walking away.

At this very moment, I wish I had a set of giddy girlfriends to call, someone who can relate to this, but all I have is David.

Oh well...

I pull my phone out of my pocket and call him.

"What's up, Pear Pear?" he answers.

"He fucked my pussy with his mouth."

"*What*?!" He sounds as if he's choking. "What did you just say?"

"The guy I'm staying with..."

"The *Blake*? You decided to stay with him the entire time? No hotel?"

"No, but that's not what I called to talk to you about." I am literally grinning from ear to ear. "He just went down on me and I fucking *loved* it!"

"We need to redefine the lines of our best friend partnership, Paris. This is so out of bounds for appropriate conversation."

"It was *amazing*! Like, more than amazing! Adrian was good, but he wasn't *memorable good* when it came to doing that to me. I mean, I usually had to force him to do it and he would only do it for like ten minutes. Did I ever tell you that?"

"Why are we still having this conversation?"

"Blake was down there for a very long time—a very, *very* long time."

"*Paris...*"

"And he made me cum! HARD! I haven't cum in over a year, and I've never cum like that before!"

"I'm very sorry to hear that." The sound of Blake's voice makes me drop the phone to the floor.

I stand completely frozen to my spot, unsure of what to say next.

"That sounded like a really interesting conversation." He walks over and picks up my phone. Then he looks into my eyes—smoothing my hair with his hands. "Good to know you thought it was *amazing*."

"I wasn't talking about you."

"Someone else made you cum within the last hour?"

I take my phone from him and turn to walk away, but he pulls me into his arms.

"Did you think of something we could do tonight?"

"We're not playing Never-Have-I Ever..."

He grins. "I wouldn't want to play that if I were you either. What do you normally do when you're stuck at home?"

"Write or catch up on work, but snowstorms don't come down south that often."

"Okay." He lets me go. "Wait here." He walks away, and I take a seat on the couch.

I honestly want to suggest a repeat of what he did to me, but I don't want to come off as needy. I guess I'll just replay the feel of his lips over and over again for the rest of my stay here.

If he's that good with his mouth, I wonder how amazing it would be if we—

"You're mumbling to yourself..." He hands me my laptop. "Do you prefer hot chocolate or coffee?"

"Hot chocolate."

He disappears again.

Minutes later, he walks into the room carrying two bright red mugs. After setting them on the table, he pulls a stack of files from the coffee table's drawer.

"Do you write with the TV on or off?" He sits next to me.

"On."

He clicks the remote, and then he pulls me close. "Are you comfortable sitting like this?"

I nod. I am absolutely speechless.

I was expecting him to return with more drinks and another game of sexual innuendos, not work. This doesn't make any sense.

"Something wrong?" He puts on a pair of reading glasses.

"No, I just thought..."

"That I would fuck you?"

"Do you always have to be so blunt? Didn't they teach you anything about social graces while you were in school?"

"Is that what you thought, Paris?" he whispers. "Tell me."

"Yes..."

He smiles, but he changes the subject. "What type of stuff do you write?"

"Reflective pieces on new laws, culture reviews, things like that." I pause. "I want to be an investigative reporter. I know I'm getting a late start on that career path, but...I've always wanted to do that."

"Your over the top suspicions make perfect sense now."

"Whatever." I laugh. "You know, I was too scared to tell Adrian my real dream after we settled in together because I didn't think he would be supportive of me having a career like that...Now that I look back, I see how crazy it is that I—" I feel his lips on mine and completely forget the rest of that sentence.

When he finally stops kissing me, he whispers against my mouth, "We're not going to talk about your ex-boyfriend for the rest of this trip. That was number two on your list, correct?"

"Yes..."

"I'm going to help you try and fulfill that one, too." He kisses my lips again. "Try to get some work done."

"Wait. Can I ask you something else?"

"You can ask me anything."

"What are your expectations as far as us?"

"What makes you think I expect anything from you?"

"Well, aside from the fact that you've assaulted my lips, fifteen minutes ago you were putting your head in my..."

"Do you know what that part of your body is called?"

"I know exactly what it's called." I still can't believe he affects me like this. "Anyway, I enjoyed it a lot and—"

"Paris..." He cups my face in his hands. "I told you that I wouldn't do anything that you didn't want to do. I meant that. If sex never happens while you're here, that's fine. If it does," he says, smiling, "*more* than fine. But I'm not going to pressure you into it. If you ever want to do that, just tell me. If not, we can just get to know each other better until it's time for you to go home."

"*Seriously?*"

He kisses my forehead. "Seriously."

Chapter 8

The snowstorm was at its worst last night. The city's power lines froze and the amount of snow that fell totaled thirteen inches. The skies were pitch black—only lightening to a dusty grey by the afternoon, and the gale force winds whipped against billboards and toppled several trees.

I'm not sure how I ended up in bed with Blake in the middle of the night, but when he'd heard me coming into his room, he immediately sat up. I'd expected him to say, "About time you admitted you wanted to fuck me," but he didn't.

Instead, he'd pulled back the covers and asked if I wanted to join him. Then, after practically beckoning me to step over to him, he wrapped his arms around me and held me close as the wind shook his windows.

"Over one hundred thousand DC residents are currently without power this morning," the newscaster says, making me roll over. "Emergency crews are trying their best to restore electricity as fast as they can, but if you know someone who is unable to call and report an outage, please call the number on the screen."

"Hi." Blake's green eyes meet mine.

"Hi."

"Do I need to get you a night-light for this evening? Would that help you stay in your own room?"

I cross my arms. "I wasn't scared."

"I didn't say you were." He smiles. "Though next time, you should probably knock before opening the door. Otherwise, I'll think you're someone who's trying to break in."

"Or someone who's walking in on you jacking yourself off."

"Very funny." He kisses my cheek. "It'd be even funnier if you hadn't been murmuring my name every fifteen minutes last night."

"I did not!"

"You did, but it's okay. I would never count your sleep-talk as an invite to your body—even though that's what you want."

I immediately roll out of the bed. "I'm going to go do some more writing now." I walk into the hallway and head to my room, but he follows me and takes my hand.

He leads me into the kitchen and pulls out a barstool. Then, as if that last conversation never happened, he starts to make breakfast and asks more questions about my writing.

Once we're done eating, he shows me into his private library—a large room that features ceiling high book cases, and we do our separate work while sitting next to each other on a couch.

Much to my surprise, the next few days pass with us following the same routine: We work sitting side by side during the afternoons, and during breaks, he insists on reading me passages from his favorite books. Of course, they're all erotic novels.

The best part of these days is the end, because for whatever reason, he feels the need to personally escort me to my room. Then he always asks, "Are you sleeping alone?"

Even though I've said yes every single time, the toe-curling kiss he gives me right after always makes me want to change my mind. And despite the fact that the storm's winds scare the hell out of me and always make me tiptoe into his bedroom in the middle of the night, he never makes a move on me.

He just holds me.

"Paris?" Blake is at my bedroom door again.

"Yes?"

"Are you sleeping alone tonight?"

I nod, and as if on cue, he presses his lips against mine and wraps his arms around my waist—kissing me harder than he's ever kissed me before.

Wrapping my arms around his neck, I murmur as he bites my bottom lip, as he rubs his hands up and down my back.

Just give in...Give the fuck in...

I pull back and fix my mouth to say, "I don't want to sleep alone," but he doesn't give me the chance. He clearly thinks me pulling away means I want to end our kiss, because he says goodnight and walks away.

"I'll be up late tonight, if you can't sleep." He looks over his shoulder.

"More case files?"

"Unfortunately," he says, and I know that "unfortunately" has a double meaning.

Chapter 9

I wake up alone in Blake's bed.

From the open windows, I can see that the snowfall has finally slowed to a few occasional flurries. The roads are still buried, but I can see emergency workers pushing mounds of it onto the sidewalks.

As I pull back the sheets, I notice a bright box on the edge of the bed that bears my name and a note: *For Tonight...*

Confused, I open the box and gasp when I see what's inside: It's a haltered silk plum dress and a pair of complementing nude heels.

"You're a six, right?" Blake steps into the room with two plates of waffles.

"Should I be offended that you've been with so many women that you can tell their sizes just by looking?"

"That, or you can be aware of the fact that I saw your jacket's tag on the plane. Whatever makes you feel better." He sets the food down. "I ordered it the same day you agreed to stay. The store owner was very surprised and wanted to know more about who you were."

"Did you tell him the truth?"

"I just told him that I liked you." He smiles. "Will you go out with me tonight?"

"Out *where*, Blake?" I point to the window. "Do you not see what's happening outside your window?"

"Is that a yes?"

"No." I shake my head. "It's an, '*Are you out of your mind*'?"

"I'm serious. Just trust me."

I roll my eyes. "Fine. What time should I be ready?"

"Eight. I'll even come to your door."

"How gentleman-like of you. Are you trying to butter me up?"

"I'm trying to do whatever it takes to get into your pants so I can finally fuck you. You're taking too long to make up your mind."

WHAT?!

I open my mouth to respond, but he kisses me before I get the chance.

"I'm joking," he whispers. "Don't look at me like that." He motions for me to sit on the bed, and then he grabs a book from his drawer.

"Now," he says, opening it. "Where did I leave off in our reading yesterday?"

"The part where the girl learned how to give the guy a blow job for the first time."

"Right..." He flips a page. "Did I get to the part where he comes in her mouth yet?"

"*Yes.*" I stuff a waffle into my mouth.

"No, I didn't." He laughs and sits next to me, putting his arm around my shoulders. "Let's pick up right there, shall we?" He clears his throat and reads. "The tip of his dick tasted salty and sweet. No, it was *sweet and salty.* Like a burnt M&M."

"Really though?"

"Yes. *Really though.* This is one of my all-time favorite books." He slides his reading glasses over his eyes. "I wasn't sure what to do next. His cock was so big, and my pussy was *so* small..."

At seven thirty, I look myself over in the bedroom's wall-length mirror.

My jet black hair is falling in loose ringlets over my shoulders, and the plum dress is hugging my small curves perfectly.

I can't imagine where he's taking me in this type of weather, and I'm hoping he's smart enough to know that we shouldn't be going out at all.

Maybe we'll just sit in front of his fireplace and drink...

"Paris?" Blake knocks on my door, and I immediately open it.

"You're wearing a tuxedo?" I try not to stare at him too hard. I swear there's nothing he doesn't look good in.

He doesn't answer my question. He looks me up and down and gently trails his finger against my exposed collarbone. "You look beautiful, Paris."

"*Beautiful*? That must be a new—"

He cuts me off with a kiss and pulls me close. Not letting me catch my breath, he whispers, "I'm being serious...You're fucking stunning."

I nod, unable to say the words "Thank you," because he can't seem to stop kissing me.

When he finally lets me go, he stares at me—looking as if he wants to say something more, but he doesn't.

He simply takes my hand and leads me into his private library, and then up a flight of side stairs that I've never noticed before.

When we reach the top, he opens a metal door and ushers me inside of what appears to be an indoor garden. The room is enclosed in plated glass; ivies are artfully crawling up the walls, and there are rows and rows of roses and tulips growing in beautiful clear cases.

On the other side of the room is a white-clothed table set for two, and a shiny silver speaker that's playing soft music.

He walks me over to it and pulls out my chair. "Have a seat."

After he pushes me closer to the table, he sits across from me. "Do you eat steak?"

I shake my head.

"I thought so." He motions for me to open the silver covered platter in front of me. "It's chicken parmesan and pasta salad."

My mouth waters as I look over the food. "Why didn't you tell me this room was up here before?"

"It didn't cross my mind until yesterday."

"Is this where you normally take your dates when they come over? When the weather is better, do you fuck them against the windows for all of your neighbors to see?"

He says nothing. He just looks at me.

"I was just joking...I didn't mean to offend you."

Still nothing.

"Blake?" I put my fork down. "I really didn't mean anything by that. I was just—"

"What do I have to do to get you to stay with me for another week?" He cuts me off. "Name it."

"*What?*"

"I want you to stay with me for another week. How can I make that happen?"

"Um..." I feel butterflies fluttering in my chest.

He reaches over the table and puts his hand over mine, waiting for a response.

"Why would you want me to stay?"

"You're the first company I've had at my house for this long in years," he says. "I also happen to *like* you and your smart-ass mouth, and I want to spend more time with you. I'll pay for your new flight ticket if that's what you're worried about."

I'm not sure what to say. I would've never expected him to say something like this.

I mean, I've really enjoyed his company as well, and I feel like his playfulness is something that I've never experienced with anyone else, but staying? If I agreed to another week, I'd never want to leave, and I'd probably start fantasizing about a relationship that'll be doomed from the start.

"Why would it be doomed from the start?" he asks.

"Huh?"

"You said if you stayed with me, you'd start fantasizing about a relationship that would be doomed from the start. What makes you think that?"

I gasp. "I was *thinking* that. I didn't mean to say it aloud."

"Well, you did." He stands—still holding onto my hand, and pulls his chair next to me. "Why do you think that?"

"Besides the obvious fact that I literally just met you, and I just got out of a relationship?"

"It was a dead relationship. Those types don't count."

"How would *you* know?"

"Divorce clients." He smiles and presses his forehead against mine. "I can do long-distance...Or you can move."

"I just met you *last week*!"

"So?"

"*So*, that's fucking crazy. You and I have just been hanging out indoors every day. That's not something you can build a relationship on."

"So I have to save you from walking into a moving bus just to get you to spend more time with me?"

I laugh. "No, but...I can't stay." For some reason, saying that hurts a little. "I mean, a big part of me wants to, but—"

"You can't." He finishes for me. Then he quickly changes the subject. "I spent a lot of time cooking that dinner. Are you going to eat it?"

"Are you going to *let* me eat it? It's kind of impossible to do when you keep talking."

He smiles and picks up my fork, stabbing a few pasta noodles, then he lifts it to my lips.

As I close my mouth around the food, his eyes light up and he whispers, "Try not to use your teeth. I need to keep this visual for long after you leave."

I don't get a chance to laugh before he pulls me into his lap and kisses my lips.

"Let's try this again," he says, preparing another forkful of noodles. "This time, look like you're really enjoying it..."

Blake walks me to my bedroom and wraps his arms around my waist. He gently pulls a bobby pin from my hair—letting a few ringlets fall in front of my forehead.

Pushing them away, he looks into my eyes. "Are you sleeping alone tonight?"

The question hangs in the air for what feels like an eternity.

I only have a few days left with him and I want to say no, I need to say no, but I can't get my mouth to say a single word.

"Paris..." he rubs his hands against my bare back, running his thumb against the zipper of my dress. "Are you sleeping alone tonight?"

"Um..."

"*Yes?*"

"Yes..." I manage, and I notice a hint of sadness in his eyes.

He whispers "Okay," and kisses me until I can't breathe, until I absolutely regret giving him the wrong fucking answer.

Slowly tearing his mouth away from mine, he sighs. "I'll be up late again. Let me know if you need anything."

"Another night of case files?"

"*Blue balls.*" He smiles and kisses my cheek. "Goodnight, Paris."

I slip into my room and silently curse myself.

I have no idea what the hell is wrong with me.

Adrian is out of the picture—has technically been for at least a year, and I want to have sex with Blake.

I want him to fuck me out of my mind like he claims he can—and I need to stop wasting my time. I made those resolutions for a reason, and I want to be able to put a checkmark next to every last one of them.

Taking a deep breath, I tell myself that time is getting shorter by the second, and I have nothing left to lose. I walk over to the closet and change into one of the silk slips that he bought me. Then I head over to his bedroom.

Opening the door, I expect to see him reading over more case files, but he isn't. He isn't even here.

I'm about to walk out and search the rest of his house, but I hear a faint sound coming from behind his bathroom walls.

"Blake?" I knock on the door.

No answer.

I step inside and raise my eyebrow at the sight in front of me. Blake's wrapping a towel around his waist and pressing his head against the wall, sighing.

I try to step back and wait for him in his bedroom, but he suddenly turns around and looks at me—smiling. "This is what you consider *sleeping alone?*"

"No..." I hesitate. "I was um...I was going to tell you that..."

"*Yes?*" His smile widens.

"I was going to ask if you could tell me where to find those coffee packets you bought. I want to make some coffee since I can't sleep...It um, makes me feel good."

"*Coffee* makes you feel good?"

I can't answer. I'm too busy focusing on the way he's looking at me, the way his towel is hanging off his waist.

"It's in the left drawer on the island. Would you like me to show it to you?"

"The coffee?"

"Yes," he says. "*The coffee.*"

"Um..." Watching him run his hands through his hair is something I could do all day. "No, that's alright. I think I can find it on my own..." I stand there for a few more seconds, telling myself to step forward and end this charade, but no words come out of my mouth.

I turn away and leave the room, sighing as I shut the door behind me. There is no way I can tell him what I really want. Hell, I've never told anyone what I really wanted.

I step out into the hallway, but before I can make my way to my room, I feel Blake wrapping his arms around me from behind.

"Did you really come to me to ask about coffee?" he whispers.

"Yes..."

He kisses the back of my neck. "I don't believe you."

I don't believe me either... "You should."

He laughs softly and tightens his grip on my waist. "Tell me you want me."

"I want *your coffee*."

He lets me go and spins me around, pressing my back against a wall. "Paris..." He tugs on the bow of my slip and looks into my eyes. "*Tell me you want me.*"

I can't speak. My heart is seconds away from falling out of my chest and all my thoughts have dissolved.

As if he can sense that I'm incapable of talking, he gently presses his lips against mine, whispering, "*Say it.*"

"Yes..." I feel his hands slipping underneath the silk and cupping my breasts.

"*Yes*, you want me, or *yes* I have to ask you to say it again?"

I suck in a breath as he presses his dick against my thigh, as he lowers his head and kisses my neck.

"Yes..." I whisper. "Yes, I...I want you."

His lips suddenly land on mine and he loops his arms around my waist, gently lifting me off the floor.

Consumed by his kiss, I wrap my legs around him— murmuring as he carries me back into his room. Without taking his lips off mine, he reaches into a drawer and pulls out a condom.

He bites my bottom lip hard before setting me down onto the floor—keeping his eyes locked on mine as he puts it on.

I'm panting, trembling in anticipation, and as he pulls me close again, I tilt my chin up to continue our kiss, but he spins me around and bends me over.

Before I can take another breath, he slides his dick into me—making me scream.

"Is this how you want to be fucked?" he whispers, pulling me back by my hair, forcing himself into me again and again.

"Yessss!" I brace my hands against the floor, trying to steady myself, but it's no use. He's controlling this—he's controlling *me*, and he's not letting me set the pace.

As I give in, he grips my waist and slowly moves me upright, never stopping his thrusts. His hands move up to my breasts and squeeze my nipples, pinching them so hard that I cry out even louder. I feel his lips on the back of my neck, feel his teeth digging into my skin, and I damn near lose control.

"Blake..."

"Yes?" One of his hands trails past my stomach—straight to my clit. Using his thumb, he gently circles it as he continues to pound into me. "You said something?"

"*Fuck, Blake...*"

"*Fuck me?*" He stops mid thrust. He grabs my hair and tilts my head back. "Is that what you said?"

My breathing is erratic. I can't get a single word out, so I simply shake my head.

"You're not enjoying this?" He pulls out of me. "I'm not fucking you rough enough?"

"No..." I try to catch my breath. "That's not what I mean...I meant—"

I don't get a chance to finish because the next thing I know, he's picking me up and tossing me over his shoulder, carrying me into the master bedroom. The one I've been occupying.

He tosses me onto the bed, and then he pulls me to the edge by my legs. "I'm not doing this right?"

"Blake..." My chest is heaving. "That's not what I meant."

"Then what did you mean?" He lifts my legs and places them around his waist.

"I meant—" I gasp as he slides into me, as he bends down to bite my nipples.

Staring into my eyes, he doesn't say another word. He slides deeper and deeper, and with each scream I let out, he squeezes my ass.

There are no kisses, no soft caresses, no sweet murmurs from his mouth. He's just fucking me.

And I'm loving every second of it.

I moan each time he slaps my skin with his palm, each time he tells me I "feel so fucking good," and each time he prevents me from taking control.

As tremors start to build inside of me and my legs start to shake, I shut my eyes. I try to pull away from him, try to move my legs from around his waist, but he doesn't let me.

He holds my thighs in place and kisses my stomach—licking his way from my navel to my breasts, and before he can reach my lips, I let go. Screaming.

My body is shaking in ways I can't even begin to explain, and no matter how hard I try to control it, I can't. I'm coming again and again and again, and he's still torturing me with his tongue, still holding my legs captive.

Shit...

I feel his release shortly after, and then I feel him collapsing on top of me.

Seconds later, he rolls off me and stands up—walking away.

He's leaving? Just like that?

I'm too elated to be upset right now, but once this euphoria wears off, the "wham, bam, thank you, ma'am" realization may hurt a little.

On my back, I scoot across the mattress until my head hits the headboard. I'm about to shut my eyes and replay what just happened, but I feel Blake sliding into bed next to me.

He wraps his arms around my waist and pulls me on top of him. "Does that take care of numbers five and eight?"

"I don't think so."

"Why not?"

"I didn't have an orgasm."

"You had *four*."

I blush. "Yes...That should um, take care of those numbers..."

"Good to know." He smiles and brushes a strand of hair away from my face. "Are you sore?"

"A little..."

Kissing my lips, he grabs my hand and slides it down his thigh—placing it onto his hardened dick.

I gasp as he uses my hand to rub it up and down.

"Now that I've fucked you *your way*, can I fuck you mine?"

My eyes widen. I'm honestly not sure if I can go another round with him, especially if it's anything half as intense.

"It's not." He's getting really good at reading my mind. He reaches over to the nightstand and pulls out a condom, handing it to me.

I take my time unwrapping it, avoiding his eyes even though I can feel him staring at me. I sit up and place it over him, trying to think of something to say in this moment, but there's no use.

The second I'm done, he grabs me and rolls me on top of him. Slightly lifting me up by my waist, he positions me over his dick and I slowly sink onto him.

I moan once he's entirely inside of me, and place my hands against his chest to steady myself.

He holds my waist still so I can't move, and then he caresses my face. "Go slow."

As his hands move away, I start to rock against him—never breaking eye contact, never wanting to.

He slides a hand around my neck and pulls my head down to his, slowly kissing me. Gently biting my bottom lip, he groans as I start to move a little faster.

"Slow, Paris..." He lets go of my lip and cups one of my breasts—circling my nipple with his tongue.

"I..." I can't go slow with him. He feels too good.

He trails his tongue to my other breast and grips my hips—preventing me from moving as fast as I want to.

"*Blake...*"

He looks into my eyes as he moves me up and down his dick, ignoring my pleas to speed things up.

"Why are you in such a rush?" He holds me still after bringing me back down, after he's completely inside of me. "Does this not feel good?"

"*Yes...*" I try to move myself back up, but his grip is too strong. "*Yes...*"

"We already fucked *your way*, didn't we?" He sits up—keeping me still, keeping us entwined. "Isn't it my turn?"

"Blake, please..." I feel him slightly moving me up—teasing me.

"Please *what*?" His hand caresses my back. "Fuck you faster?"

I nod, but he doesn't oblige. He presses his mouth against my neck—softly biting my skin whenever I say his name.

He rocks me against his dick again and I start to tremble—start to quiver in anticipation of a release, but each time I get close, he stops and kisses my lips instead.

"*Please...*" I murmur as he runs his fingers through my hair.

Kissing me, he finally lets my waist go and I wrap my arms around his neck.

I grind my hips into his, letting the tremors build and build—letting his lips continue to make love to my mouth.

"*Ohhh....Godddd...I...*" My skin slaps against his one last time and I lose all control. "*Blake...*"

I fall forward—knocking us both to the mattress. I can hear him saying words, but I can't understand them over my heavy breathing.

Seemingly concerned, he lifts me off of him and lays me on the other side of the bed.

"Paris?" He sweeps sweaty strands of hair away from my forehead. "Are you okay?"

I try to say, "Fuck yes," but everything goes black.

My body is sore. Beyond sore.

I can barely feel my legs, my arms are weary, and the skin on my neck is reeling from all the sensual bites Blake placed there.

I don't want to get up for the rest of the day. I just want to lie here—against Blake's chest, and relive every single second of last night.

I've never been fucked like that. Ever.

I suddenly feel his hands rubbing my back and my eyes flutter open.

"Good morning." He smiles.

"Good morning..."

He pulls me close and kisses my forehead. "Are you feeling okay?"

I nod.

Gently, he slides his hands to my hips and pulls me even closer. "Did you have any plans in mind for today?"

"Has the snow magically gone away?"

"No."

"Then I don't have that many options, do I?"

"I have an idea." He traces my lips with his fingers.

"I'm sure you do."

"It's not what you think it is."

"Oh..." I'm actually sad that it isn't.

"I'm going to make you breakfast while you shower, and then I'm going to take you somewhere."

"Aren't the roads still bad?"

"They are." He rolls out of the bed. "Go shower."

"*Alone?*" I gasp once I realize that I've said that aloud.

"Yes, alone." He looks over my body. "If I shower with you, we won't get anything else done today."

I'm not sure why that's such a bad thing, but I don't get a chance to ask him about it. By the time I realize that he's serious about me taking a shower alone, he's left the room.

I lift myself up from the bed and make my way into the bathroom—smiling at every muscle ache that I currently feel. I'm not sure how I manage to get into his shower, but I'm honestly incapable of doing anything past turning on the water.

I stand still and let the streams fall over me—sighing every few minutes, asking myself if staying with him for a few more days would really ruin anything. I've had more fun with him these past few days than I had with Adrian in the last three years combined.

As the glass begins to fog, I shut my eyes and hold my face under the water for what feels like forever. I don't want to think about anything but last night, and I honestly hope that all Blake has planned is a repeat.

I'm replaying the part where he kissed me against the wall, when I feel hands cupping my breasts from behind.

I immediately open my eyes and turn around to see Blake.

"I thought you said no to showering together?"

"I changed my mind." He covers my lips with his and pushes me against the wall. "I'm going to fuck you again."

He tries to lift my leg around his waist, but I don't let him. I tear my lips away from his mouth and start to plant kisses against his chest.

As he threads his fingers through my hair, I move my kisses down to his abs, then to his stomach.

I look up at him as I gently rub his dick, as I tease his tip with my tongue—listening to the light groans that are escaping from his mouth.

"*Paris...*"

I swirl my tongue all around him, ignoring how roughly he's pulling my hair.

"*Fuck...*" He yanks me up and spins me around—pressing my breasts against the tile. "I'll take you out tomorrow..."

Chapter 10

Three days left.

That's it.

That's all I have left with Blake and for some reason, I'm dreading saying goodbye. I figure he must be dreading it as well, because he's been asking me what it'll take for me to stay every chance he gets.

He's told me to wear something casual so he can take me out again, so I'm wearing jeans and a red T-shirt.

As I look over myself in the mirror, my phone rings. David.

"Hello?"

"Am I interrupting another pussy-licking session or are you able to talk?"

"I'm able to talk." I roll my eyes. "But only for a few minutes. He's taking me out tonight...*again*."

"Of course he is." He laughs. "Could you do me a fucking favor and call your mom, please? She's been calling me every hour on the hour because you have yet to call her back. It's been over a week, Paris. Don't you find that a bit irresponsible on your part?"

I frown. I've ignored every other person that's called me since I came here; I don't want to face the drama that's waiting for me in Nashville any time soon.

"I don't want to talk to her, David. Or anyone else for that matter. They all just want me to apologize to Adrian and take him back. I can't do that."

"Wow."

"Wow? Wow, *what*?"

"Nothing, I just..." He pauses. "I think I actually believe that you won't take him back this time."

"And why is that?"

"Normally, whenever you argue with him and 'break-up', you say 'I won't' go back to him but you always do. It's quite refreshing to hear you say, *I can't.*" He sounds extremely proud. "Letting go of him was long overdue, but I'm looking forward to finally seeing you happy again."

"Thanks a lot, David," I say. "Can I tell you something?"

"Does it involve what I think it involves?"

"We had sex the other night." I have to tell him this. He *has* to know. "More than once! And it was rough and hot, and just...It was good! Like, so amazingly good!"

"*Paris...*"

"I didn't want him to ever stop! It was just—I'm actually getting wet just thinking about it... It was like one of those stories you tell me about your hot one night stands, but it was me. It was *me*, David! And guess what else?"

"What else, Pear Pear?"

"His dick is huge..."

He sighs loudly.

"I wasn't sure if I'd ever be able to go down on him because I didn't think it'd fit into my mouth, but it did! And I think he enjoyed how far it was down my throat. Like, at first he was telling me to suck him slow so—"

There was a loud and sudden beep on the other end.

"David?" I listen for him. "*David*? David, are you there?" I look at my phone and see that he's sent a text:

Love you Pear, Pear. Glad you're having fun. Call me when you don't want to talk about another man's dick.

Laughing, I place the phone into a drawer. I'm not going to use it again until it's time to leave; I want to focus on the remaining time I have left with Blake.

"Paris?" Blake steps into the room. "Are you ready?"

I nod and he helps me into my jacket. Clasping my hand, he walks me through his house and into the garage.

"Blake, the roads are still bad. Why are we getting into your car?"

He doesn't answer. He just motions for me to sit in the passenger seat.

As soon as he gets behind the wheel, he cranks the engine and turns on the heat. "Are you comfortable?"

"Do you have a death wish, Blake?" I cross my arms. "Because I don't. You heard the newscasters say that the roads aren't completely salted yet."

"We're not taking any roads."

"We're just going to sit here?"

"Not exactly." He leans over and kisses me, pulling up the emergency brake. "I'm going to kiss you until you can't breathe, and then I'm going to fuck you in the backseat."

"This is what you consider *a date*?"

"I never said this was a date."

"You said you were taking me out."

"Out as in *outside*. Are we not outside?"

As much as I want to punch him in the face right now, I can't help but laugh. "You are really something. Do you know that? This is probably why you've never had a girlfriend."

"If I had one, she would always drink during Never Have I Ever, because I would make sure that we kiss and have sex *everywhere*..." He caresses my cheek with the back of his hand. "I would never be patient enough to wait for privacy."

I blush and he kisses me again, moving to my side of the car. Whispering, he slowly unzips my jacket. "Is there anything I can say to make you stay for another week?"

I shake my head.

"Are you sure?"

I suck in a breath and murmur, "Yes," as he unclips my bra.

"Well in that case..." He unfastens my jeans. "Let's see if there's something I can *do* instead..."

Chapter 11

I don't want to leave Washington. Ever.

I want to stay here and have sex with Blake all day, every day, but I know that's impossible. Unrealistic.

What happened between the two of us over the past week and a half is something I'll always remember, but something I can't let last.

The storm is over and he has a firm to run.

I have a life to rebuild. Sooner rather than later.

Maybe that's why neither of us has said a word to each other this morning, and the glances we've stolen from one another haven't lasted for more than a second.

I'm not sure how many times I've double checked my bag—knowing damn well that I have everything. I'm just stalling because this isn't as easy as I thought it would be.

Earlier this morning, when we woke up, Blake had left me one last gift on the nightstand. It was a small grey box and inside were two items: A flight ticket to Nashville that was scheduled to leave in four days with the words, "Stay," written across the top. And a small charm—a small silver plane with the words "You're in my seat" etched onto its wings.

I'd wanted to take them both, to tell him "okay" to me staying, but I couldn't do it. Instead, I slipped the charm onto my bracelet and wrote the words, "I can't..." on the flight ticket.

"I'm ready now," I say when I walk into the living room.

"Okay." He stands up from the couch and takes my bag from me, leading the way to the garage. He looks over at me once before he pulls off, saying, "I enjoyed every second that you were here."

"Me, too."

We don't talk on the way to the airport. There's nothing to say.

I look over at him every chance I get, trying to make sure I memorize his every feature, and every time he looks at me I pretend as if I wasn't staring.

When we make it to the airport, he grabs my bag and opens my door—walking me inside like a complete and total gentleman.

Taking my bag from him, I avoid eye contact. "Thank you so much for letting me stay with you, Blake. I really appreciate it."

"You're welcome."

"And um...The sex was okay."

He places his fingers underneath my chin and tilts my head up. "*Okay?*"

"Do I need to define the word for you?"

He slips his arms around my waist and presses his lips against mine. "I'm sure you'll still be thinking about how 'okay' it was weeks from now."

"Maybe."

Hugging me a little tighter, he sighs. "What's the worst that could happen if you stayed with me for four more days?"

I open my mouth to say, "Nothing" but I pause. "*Feelings.*"

Not seeming to understand the ramifications behind that, he kisses my forehead—whispering, "I wouldn't mind that." And then he lets me go.

I turn around and walk away from him, but I stop and look over my shoulder.

He looks absolutely confused—torn, but he's hiding it behind a smile.

I walk over to him again, wrapping my arms around his neck and kissing him like he's kissed me so many times before. "Thank you for everything."

"You've already told me that." He pulls away and threads his fingers through my hair.

"So?"

"*So*, if you still plan on leaving me, I suggest you do it now because if you don't, I'll be dragging you back home within the next twenty seconds."

"Goodbye, Blake." I slowly let go of him and head towards the desk, looking back every few seconds—making sure he's still watching me. Until he isn't anymore.

For some reason, my chest is tightening, and I can't help but feel like I'm making a huge mistake.

"Welcome back, Miss Weston," the desk agent says as she hands me my boarding pass. "Have a safe flight."

I look over my shoulder, telling myself that if Blake is still there, it must be some type of hopeless romantic sign, but he isn't. No one is.

I make my way through security without incident. There are no random alarms, no TSA agents emptying and re-emptying my bag, and unfortunately, no one I'm in a rush to get away from this time.

By the time I make it to my gate, almost everyone has boarded.

"Enjoy first class, Miss Weston." A woman scans my ticket, and I smile.

I'd told Blake that my ticket home was coach-class and that I didn't need an upgrade, but he's done it anyway. I want to send him a text, to playfully berate him for going against what I said, but I can't.

I don't want him to get the wrong impression.

We've already said goodbye.

As I buckle my seatbelt, I look outside my window. I'm halfway expecting Blake to come on board at any second, to say, "I've decided I want to fuck you in Nashville, too," but no one takes the seat next to me.

"Ladies and gentlemen aboard flight number 3718, the main cabin doors will be closing in two minutes..."

I tap my foot in anticipation, still holding on to the same hope.

"The main cabin doors have officially been closed. Please stow away all personal electronic devices until we reach the proper altitude."

I shut my eyes and lean back in my seat. The second Blake's face crosses my mind, I know for a fact that I've made a big ass mistake.

I could've stayed for four more days...

I bypass baggage claim and make my way to the escalators.

As the steps descend, I see David standing in line with the other sign holders. He's written "Pear Pear" in red marker and drawn what appears to be a tongue and a vagina underneath it.

"*Seriously?*" I snatch the sign away from him. "Why are we friends?"

"I have no idea." He laughs and takes my bag. "How were the last few days of your trip? Please withhold all sex stories until I put on my headphones."

"They were okay."

"*Okay?* That's it?"

"Yeah."

"What happened to all the 'OMG-his dick actually fits into my mouth' excitement?"

"Really, David?" I shake my head. "I enjoyed it. We pretty much had sex over and over again. Oh and we watched a few terrible movies in between him cooking for me."

He stops walking and puts his hands on my shoulders. "You *like* him, don't you?"

"Do not. I barely know him. The sex was just really good and we understood each other's sarcasm."

A little too well...

"Call him and ask if he can come visit you sometime. It's not like you have anything else to do on the weekends. Plus, you're practically homeless and unemployed right now."

"Am I not staying at your place anymore? We're not going to hang out on the weekends?"

"Not at night." He scoffs. "You'll need to stay on your side of the house whenever I have company. As a matter of fact, I amended one of my resolutions just for you."

"Your number eleven?"

"You're not *that* special. I can't remember what number, but it said, "Help Paris find female friends to discuss dicks with." If I don't make any of the other ones, I'm definitely going to make that one happen." He leads me to the parking garage.

Today he's driving his black Mercedes and I can't help but think about Blake...

"What are the benefits of having a boyfriend?" Blake kisses my lips.

"I'm the worst person to ask right now. Don't you think?"

"You said things were great in the beginning. How so?"

I smile as he moves on top of me. "Um...Well, you can talk to that person about any and everything, and he won't judge you. He's your shoulder to cry on whenever you need it...He remembers all the little things that make you happy on your worst days and vice versa. You're completely comfortable with him and...You know, there's unlimited physical stuff..."

"Sex?"

"Kisses." I roll my eyes. "Yes, sex."

"It sounds intriguing."

"Intriguing enough for you to actually try it one day?"

"Maybe." He runs his hand across my thighs. "If I found the right woman."

"Make sure you hide all of your true colors when you first meet."

"Why would I do that?"

"Because if you show her who you really are, if she knows how blunt you are and that you don't have a filter, you might ruin your chances after a first encounter."

He laughs and grabs a condom from the dresser. "We'll see..."

"You really do like this guy, huh?" The sound of David's laughter cuts through my memories, and I realize we're on the expressway.

"No. The sex was just *that* good." I lie. "I'll be sure to fill you in on all the details later."

"Please don't."

"Whatever. Hey, you didn't tell me the rest of your resolutions yet. Spill."

"No, thanks. I've repeated them to your mother countless times over the past three days. When you finally decide to call her back, you can ask her all about them."

I roll my eyes.

"You, however," he says, "can read me yours so I can pretend like I care."

Smiling, I pull out my wallet and unfold my list.

I rattle off numbers one through seven—ignoring David's request to enunciate the word "orgasm" properly, and then I notice that while the next two are the same, the rest of my list has been changed:

7. Write everyday...I'm supposed to be an aspiring journalist, but this list is the first thing I've written in months. MONTHS.

(I called Vanderbilt...One of my old law professors works in admissions. Call them on Tuesday.)

*8. Have passionate, hot sex...with someone who can give
me an ORGASM...*

(I think you've satisfied this one...More than once...)

*9. Start working out...Ha! No. Scratch that...I'll come
back to number nine.*

(Start smiling more. You're too beautiful not to...)

10. And number ten, too...

**(Stop worrying about what your mom, your sister, or
the rest of your family thinks regarding your
decisions...Live your life for you.)**

11. And I still need a number eleven ...

**(Pick Blake up from the Nashville airport in four days...He
wants to make sure two of the things on this list are ALWAYS
taken care of...)**
THE END

A Letter to the Reader

<u>Dear Incredible Reader</u>,

Thank you so much for taking time out of your life to read this book! I hope you were thoroughly entertained and enjoyed reading it as much as I enjoyed writing it.

If you LOVED it and have any extra time, PLEASE leave a review on amazon.com, B&N.com, goodreads.com, OR <u>find me here on Facebook</u> so I can personally thank you :-) If you hated it, well...keep that shit to yourself! LOL (Just kidding. Feel free to let me know how I can improve next time!)

I'm forever grateful for you and your time, and I hope to be re-invited to your bookshelf with my next release. (Speaking of my next release, if you'd like to be a part of my mailing list so you can be notified of my upcoming release dates and special offers, please sign up via this <u>link.</u>)

Love,
Whitney G.

A Sneak Peek of Reasonable Doubt

By Whitney G.
Prologue

Andrew

New York City is nothing more than a shit-filled wasteland, a dump where failures are forced to drop all their broken dreams and leave them far behind. The flashing lights that shined brightly years ago have lost their luster, and that fresh feeling that once permeated the air—that *hopefulness*, is long gone.

Every person I once considered a friend is now an enemy, and the word "trust" has been ripped from my vocabulary. My name and reputation are tarnished, thanks to the press, and after reading the headline that *The New York Times* ran this morning, I've decided that tonight will be the last night I ever spend here.

I can't deal with the cold sweats and nightmares that jerk me out of my sleep anymore, and as hard as I try to pretend like my heart hasn't been obliterated, I doubt that the agonizing ache in my chest will ever go away.

To properly say goodbye, I've ordered the best entrées from all my favorite restaurants, watched *Death of a Salesman* on Broadway, and smoked a Cuban cigar on the Brooklyn Bridge. I've also booked the penthouse suite at the Waldorf Astoria, where I'm now leaning back on the bed and threading my fingers through a woman's hair—groaning as she slides her mouth over my cock.

Teasingly darting her tongue around my tip, she whispers, "Do you like this?" as she looks up at me.

I don't answer. I push her head down and exhale as she presses her lips against my balls, as she covers my cock with her hands and moves them up and down.

Over the past two hours, I've fucked her against the wall, forced her to bend over a chair, and pinned her legs to the mattress while I devoured her pussy.

It's been quite fulfilling—*fun*, but I know this feeling will only last for so long; it never stays. In less than a week, I'll have to find someone else.

As she takes me deeper and deeper into her mouth, I tightly tug her hair—tensing as she bobs her head up and down. Pleasure begins to course its way through me, and the muscles in my legs stiffen—forcing me to let go and warn her to pull away.

She ignores me.

She grips my knees and sucks faster, letting my cock touch the back of her throat. I give her one last chance to move away, but since her lips remain wrapped around me, she leaves me no choice but to cum in her mouth.

And then she swallows.

Every. Last. Drop.

Impressive...

Finally pulling away, she licks her lips and leans back against the floor.

"That was my first time swallowing," she says. "I did that just for you."

"You shouldn't have." I stand and zip my pants. "You should've saved it for someone else."

"Right. Well, um...Do you want to order some dinner? Maybe we could eat it over HBO and go at it again afterwards?"

I raise my eyebrow, confused.

This is always the most annoying part, the part when the woman who previously agreed to "One dinner. One night. No repeats." wants to establish some type of imaginary connection. For whatever reason, she feels like there needs to be some type of closure conversation, some bland reassurance that'll confirm that what just happened was 'more than sex,' and we'll become friends.

But it *was* just sex, and I'm not in need of any friends. Not now, not ever.

"No, thank you." I walk over to the mirror on the other side of the room. "I have someplace to be."

"At three in the morning? I mean, if you just want to skip the HBO and go for another round instead, I can..."

Her irritating voice fades into my thoughts, and I begin to button my shirt. I've never spent the night with a woman I met online, and she isn't going to be the first.

As I adjust my tie, I look down and spot a tattered pink wallet on the dresser. Picking it up, I flip it open and run my fingers across the name that's printed onto her license: Sarah Tate.

Even though I've only known this woman for a week, she's always answered to "Samantha." She's also told me—*repeatedly*, that she works as a nurse at Grace Hospital. Judging by the Wal-Mart employee card that's hiding behind her license, I'm assuming that part isn't true either.

I look over my shoulder, where she's now sprawled across the bed's silk sheets. Her creamy colored skin is unmarred and smooth; her bow shaped lips are slightly swollen and puffy.

Her green eyes meet mine and she slowly sits up, spreading her legs further apart, whispering, "You know you want to stay. *Stay...*"

My cock starts to harden—it's definitely up for another round, but seeing her real name has ruined any chance of that for me. I can't stand to be around someone who's lied to me, even if she does have double D tits and a mouth from heaven.

I toss the wallet into her lap. "You told me your name was Samantha."

"Okay. *And?*"

"Your name is *Sarah*."

"So what?" She shrugs, beckoning me with her hand. "I never give my real name to men I meet on the internet."

"You just fuck them in five star hotel suites?"

"Why do you suddenly care about my real name?"

"I don't." I glance at my watch. "Are you spending the night in this room or do I need to give you cab money to get home?"

"*What?*"

"Was my question unclear?"

"Wow...Just, wow..." She shakes her head. "How much longer do you think you'll be able to keep doing this?"

"Keep doing *what?*"

"Chatting someone up for a week, fucking her, and moving on to the next. How much longer?"

"Until my dick stops working." I put on my jacket. "Do you need cab fare or are you staying? Check out is at noon."

"Do you know that men like you—*relationship avoiders*, are the type that typically fall the hardest?"

"Did they teach you that at Wal-Mart?"

"Just because someone from your past hurt you, doesn't mean that every woman after her will." She purses her lips. "That's probably why you are the way you are. Maybe if you tried to actually *date* someone, you'd be a lot happier. You should take her out for dinner and actually listen, see her to her door without expecting an invitation inside, and maybe bypass the whole 'let's go fuck' in the hotel suite thing at the end."

Where are my keys? I need to go. Now.

"I can see it now..." She can't seem to shut up. "You're going to want more than sex one day, and the person you want it from is going to be someone you least expect. Someone who will force you to give in."

I pull my keys from underneath her crumpled dress and sigh. "Do you need cab money?"

"I have my own car, dick-face." She rolls her eyes. "Are you really this incapable of having a regular conversation? Would it kill you to talk to me for a few minutes after sex?"

"We have nothing more to discuss." I set my room key on the nightstand and walk toward the door. "It was very nice meeting you, Samantha, *Sarah*. Whatever the hell your name is. Have a great night."

"*Screw you*!"

"Three times was more than enough. No, thank you."

"Things are going to catch up to you one day, asshole!" She yells as I step into the hallway. "Karma is one hell of a bitch!"

"I know." I toss back. "I fucked her two weeks ago..."

Reasonable Doubt is now available in a full series boxed set!

Also by Whitney G.

To be a part of my mailing list and be notified of release dates and special offers, please sign up via this link.

Reasonable Doubt Full Series

Reasonable Doubt #1

Reasonable Doubt # 2

Reasonable Doubt #3

Mid Life Love Series:

Mid Life Love

Mid Life Love: At Last

UPCOMING WORKS

Turbulence

(Early 2016)

Twisted Love

(Spring 2016)

The Jilted Bride Series:

(Summer 2016)

Book 1: Scorned

Book 2: Tarnished

Book 3: Burned

Malpractice

(Fall 2016)

Made in the USA
Coppell, TX
20 March 2022

75292081R00066